heaven is paved with oreos

by

Catherine Gilbert Murdock

Houghton Mifflin Harcourt
Boston   New York

Houghton Mifflin Books for Children is an imprint of
Houghton Mifflin Harcourt Publishing Company.
www.hmhbooks.com
The text of this book is set in Stemple Garamond.
Library of Congress Cataloging-in-Publication Data
Murdock, Catherine Gilbert.
Heaven is paved with Oreos / by Catherine Gilbert Murdock.
p. cm.
Summary: Fourteen-year-old Sarah keeps a journal of her pilgrimage
to Rome with her eccentric grandmother, Z, her evolving relationship
with best friend Curtis, and daily conversations with Curtis's sister and
star athlete, D.J.
ISBN 978-0-547-62538-6
[1. Interpersonal relations—Fiction. 2. Pilgrims and pilgrimages—Fiction.
3. Grandmothers—Fiction. 4. Diaries—Fiction. 5. Rome (Italy)—Fiction.
6. Italy—Fiction. 7. Wisconsin—Fiction.] I. Title.
PZ7.M9415He 2013
[Fic]—dc23
2012039969

Manufactured in the U.S.A.
DOC 10 9 8 7 6 5 4 3 2 1
4500427226

To D.J.

MY JOURNAL

HELL IS PAVED WITH GOOD INTENTIONS
Heaven is paved with Oreos.

Darling Sarah!

*This journal is for you — isn't it glorious? I saw it &
thought of you instantly! Now you can record all your
thoughts & your genius & your experiences-to-come!
(And are you going to have experiences!) Some day,
when you're a creaky sixty-three-year-old granny, you'll
read this & remember every one of your marvelous
adventures. I am so excited! Have fun writing!*

Peace forever — Z

Wednesday, June 12

Wow. My very own journal. What do you write in a
journal? Because I don't really have marvelous adventures — not like my grandmother Z. My grandmother Z
could have an adventure just shopping for pencils. One
time she left her apartment to buy milk and she didn't
make it home for seventy-one hours. *That's* a marvelous
adventure. My big adventure for today was making sure
my best friend didn't throw up.

Curtis Schwenk — he's my best friend — is exceedingly shy. He does not like being the center of attention
or even the perimeter of attention. In school he never
talks at all. If he went out to buy pencils, he would be

too shy even to ask where the pencils are located and he would go home empty-handed. A huge public thing like graduation is not a place he would ever happily be, even if he was one of the people graduating, which he is not because we have only finished eighth grade.

This year, though, Curtis's older brother Win was the speaker at the Red Bend High School graduation ceremony. Curtis's brother got intensely hurt playing football last year, and now he is recovering. Crowds of people came to hear him talk about overcoming the odds and being a fighter while Curtis sat next to him onstage in a necktie looking 100% queasy. I spent the whole speech sending Curtis morally supportive brain waves.

Then they gave out diplomas and graduation was over. Everyone said congratulations to everyone else even if there was nothing to congratulate them for. I myself got four congratulations just for standing there. The fourth time, I congratulated the person right back and he did not even mind.

For a while I lost sight of Curtis, but then I found him again. Curtis is actually quite easy to find sight of because he is so tall. He saw me and smiled a huge relief-filled smile. "Hey," he said, lifting up his hand. We Palm Saluted. A Palm Salute is where one person touches his or her left palm to the other person's right palm. It is an amazingly fantastic gesture of greeting. Curtis and I invented it. We are, I think, the only people in the world who do it. Curtis's hands are so big that my fingertips only reach his middle phalanx. (That is the scientific name for the middle set of bones in your fingers. I looked it up.)

"Hey," I said, smiling at him. Every time we Palm Salute, I smile. "How's Boris?"

"Okay, I think. I haven't lifted the cover."

"How bad's the smell?"

Just then Emily Friend squeezed in next to Curtis. Note that she appeared as Curtis and I were discussing odors. "Hey, Curtis!" she said with that voice she has. "You looked very cool up there."

Curtis did not say anything. But he quickly took his eyes off me and instead stared at the ground. He would not even share an eye roll.

"Hey, Sarah." Emily always says my name as though she is just remembering it, even though we have been in school together since kindergarten. "Did you tie Curtis's necktie for him? My cousin taught me how to tie ties, and it's very important, you know, knowing how to tie your boyfriend's tie . . . If you ever need anyone to tie it for you, Curtis, I can do it. I know how." Then she gave me a look and she left. A look that means, *I don't care what everyone says: I know the truth. I'm onto you.*

Curtis kept staring at the ground. I tried to think of what I could have said back to Emily. For example: *Curtis and I would rather hang out with a dead calf than with you.* Or *Your name is Emily Friend, but you're really Emily Enemy.* But neither of these responses would work. No response works if you only think it up after the person has already left.

Finally I said, "So . . . Library? Tomorrow?"

Curtis nodded. "After practice." He looked like he wanted to say something else, but I waited and he didn't. Mom was talking to Curtis's sister, D.J. — probably saying congratulations because there weren't any graduates nearby to say it to. Paul stood behind Mom looking dazed. My brother is a little obsessed with Curtis's sister. He has articles about D.J. Schwenk playing boys' football and girls' basketball taped all over the inside of his closet. He is 100% in awe of her.

Then Curtis went off with D.J., and I went off with Mom and Paul, and Mom said Emily seemed nice because Mom = clueless. Dad was home from work by the time we got there. He asked about graduation. "In three more years," Dad said to Paul, "that will be you." He clinked his slice of pizza against Paul's, like people in movies do with champagne. "And here's to four more years for Sarah," he added, and clinked his pizza with me. Four years! That's how long it is until my very own high school graduation. I am worried about high school, but not too worried. Curtis will be there.

Z is coming for supper tomorrow night — that's why I'm writing now. She will be immensely thrilled with my journaling. She will say that watching graduation is an adventure too. Good night!

Thursday, June 13

Today I'll write until Curtis's baseball practice ends and the library opens and we can go work on Boris. It's either write or listen to Paul practice guitar. I have < 0.00% interest in that.

Curtis Schwenk and I didn't used to be best friends. We were always in the same grade, but we moved in different circles because he is exceptionally athletic and I am exceptionally not. You could say Curtis moved in circles and I moved in uncoordinated blobs.

Then one day at recess in seventh grade I found a dead robin. I should have ignored it, because whenever I pay attention to things like that, it always ends badly. Which happened this time too. I was not even touching the robin but only studying it when three boys came by.

"That's disgusting!" said Brett Ortlieb. "Kick it!"

I tried to stop them, because nothing that was once

alive should be kicked, but my blocking them only made them try harder while Emily Enemy and her friends made grossed-out expressions at me.

That's when Curtis showed up. He was the tallest kid in school even in seventh grade. All of a sudden he was leaning over Brett and staring at him. "Stop," he said. One word.

"It's a *dead bird!*" Brett said. "It's disgusting."

Curtis didn't say anything, but he clenched his fists. Even if you were looking only at his face, you could see the clenching. He stared at Brett, and Brett stared back until finally Brett muttered "whatever," and he and his friends walked away.

I stood there. So did Curtis. At last I said, "I was trying to figure out how it died."

Curtis studied me like he thought I was teasing him. Then he pointed to the gym windows. They were shiny and high — bird high. The robin must have flown into the window and broken its neck.

"Oh," I said. "I should have figured that out."

At that moment the bell rang and we had to go inside. Curtis was late, though, I noticed. He didn't show up until ten minutes into class. Out of the corner of my eye I watched him sit down. He was holding something longish, with dirt stuck to one end. It was a ruler, I could see finally. He slipped it into his backpack.

Curtis had buried the robin. He had dug a hole with a ruler and buried it. Which is exactly what I would have done . . . but I never would have been brave enough to be late to class to do it.

I was so impressed by all this that I did not think about anything else for the entire rest of the day.

A few weeks later, Curtis and I ended up partners for a big project on the scientific elements. We picked hydrogen because it is number 1 (that is a chemistry joke). Curtis brought in pictures of the Hindenburg, which is a famous zeppelin from the 1930s that caught fire because it was filled with hydrogen, which burns extremely easily. When hydrogen burns, it turns into water — and yet the water doesn't put the fire out! Even as Curtis was showing me the pictures and talking about it, he was so shy that he kept stopping, and I was so psyched about his pictures that he looked like he thought I was teasing. Then he was pleased. He tried to hide it, but I could tell.

Our display was amazing. I will not lie. We had models of hydrogen and H_2 (because hydrogen likes being in pairs) and H_2O (water) and H_2O_2 (hydrogen peroxide), and video of the Hindenburg burning, and the formula H_2 (hydrogen) + O_2 (oxygen) = H_2O (water) + O (oxygen) + heat (burning zeppelin). Our project was so amazing that a high school teacher told us we should make something for the science fair. So last year we made "Desiccation and Its Effects" using dried rats from Curtis's family's farm, and we came in third in the state! Also we started going out.

Now we are preparing for the high school state science fair, which is a much bigger deal because we will be only lowly freshmen. Our project is "Skeletal Taxidermy and Bovine Osteology: The Process of Discovery." We are assembling the skeleton of a calf from Schwenk Farm that was born dead. Out of respect we have named him Boris, and we have put him in a burial chamber with lots of dirt over him for the worms and ants and other decay-positive life forms, and a cover on top of the burial chamber so coyotes don't get to him, and now we are waiting for nature to do her work and eat up everything but the bones. It will take about two months, we think. In the meantime we are making the rest of the exhibit.

I am extremely certain Emily could never prepare a calf skeleton. I am not so certain that Curtis thinks that's a bad thing.

Thursday, June 13 — LATER

Curtis and I work at the Red Bend Library. The children's librarian likes me because I try to read every book in the kids' section, so we get to use a For Library Use Only room that is closed to the public because it does not have exit signs.

Today we spent two hours talking about which pictures to use in the science fair display and what the text blocks should say. We had our usual discussion about what is scientific versus what is gross, which both of us have a problem with. We tend not to notice the grossness. Is it gross to have a "before" photograph of poor little Boris? We are not sure.

At one point Curtis said, "What would Emily Friend think?"

I know he was only bringing up someone who is the opposite of scientific, and I tried not to mind that he used her when there are so many other people to name . . . But I will be honest and say that it hurt my feelings. Because for one thing, Emily finds everything gross, particularly everything related to me, and also she is Emily Enemy.

It did not help that after we finished and put our papers away and walked back to my house, we passed Emily Enemy herself with several other kids hanging out on the bench for the cool kids (= kids who think they're cool). Emily was sitting on one boy's lap with her legs on another boy's lap, and she said hello to Curtis but not a word to me. Actually, that is not true: she said, "You two are very cute together!" But she laughed when she said it.

We did not laugh. Curtis scowled at the ground, and I wanted to say how not every girl needs to lie across two boys just to show she's popular. I wish I could beat her at chess and make that the end of it. Is everyone in high school going to be like Emily?

Curtis and I did not say anything else for the rest of the walk.

When we got to my house, Curtis's sister's car was parked in front of our sidewalk. She wasn't in the car, though. The only person visible was my brother, who was on our front steps looking 100% miserable.

"Wow," I said. "What's wrong?" Curtis went over to the garage and started shooting baskets. Curtis does not like "what's wrong?" conversations.

Paul looked at me with crazy wide-open eyes. "You know those guitar lessons Z set up? Mom hired *her* to drive me to Prophetstown!" He grabbed my arm. "D.J. Schwenk!"

"D.J. Schwenk is driving to Prophetstown?" Prophetstown is where Z lives.

"She's got some basketball thing there . . . Help me, Sarah. I can't sit in a car with D.J. Schwenk."

I wanted to be sympathetic — Paul looked so upset! — but I could not help being reasonable. Reasonableness is the byproduct of a scientific mind. "Paul, Prophetstown is, like, forty-five minutes away. If Mom drives, that's an hour and a half twice a week — "

"Plus dog walking," Paul added. "Z wants me to walk Jack Russell George."

"Jack Russell George?" Paul doesn't even like Jack Russell George!

"Trust me, I don't want the money — "

"You're getting paid to walk Jack Russell George?" Walking Jack Russell George would be such a great job for someone who loves dogs (= me)! It's not like I have anything better to do this summer — all I'm doing is reading and baby-sitting and waiting for Boris to decay. "That is so unfair! I'm the one who should be walking him — "

Suddenly I stopped talking because a fantastic idea came into my head — and from the expression on his face I could see that the same fantastic idea came into Paul's head too. We looked at each other. "Could you — ?" Paul asked, just as I said, "I could — " We went inside.

There was D.J. Schwenk in our kitchen, sitting in Dad's chair with a pop and a bowl of ice cream and talking about a basketball club she's playing in this summer. Mom was listening while also reading the cookbook Z gave her on wheat-free desserts. Mom seemed a lot more interested in D.J. than in the cookbook.

Paul saw D.J. and stopped short. I did too. Curtis's sister is exceedingly intimidating. I mean, she is a nice person — nice to me and nice to Curtis, and last year when Paul was a freshman and some kid was picking on him, she beat that kid up with one hand. That's the thing: she is nice, but she is tough. She is so tough that she plays varsity football with boys. She was MVP at the girls' basketball state tournament this year and already has a full scholarship to play basketball at the University of Minnesota, even though she still has a year of high school left. When she walks onto a basketball court, she looks like a lion picking out which zebra to eat for dinner.

D.J. saw us and grinned. "Hi, Sarah. Hey, Paul. How are ya?"

"Hi, D.J.," Paul said with enormous effort. "Um, Sarah, can you, um, ask them . . . ?"

"Hey, D.J. Hey, Mom. Um, what would you think — what if I walked Jack Russell George?"

"So she could ride to Prophetstown with me and" — Paul made a strangling sound — "D.J.?"

"Huh," Mom said. She frowned in a not-a-bad-idea kind of way. "D.J., you okay taking Sarah, too? Oh, cripes, I don't have oat flour."

D.J. smiled. You can tell she likes Paul. "Car's going to the same place . . . But you're not going to talk about that calf, are you?"

I shook my head. Curtis and I have learned that hardly any people share our thirst for knowledge when it comes to dead things.

Now I get to go to Prophetstown and walk Jack Russell George!

Prophetstown is hugely different from Red Bend. It has art galleries and yoga and a cool hippie restaurant called Harmony Coffee where you can sit for hours without ordering anything and a street named after Laura Ingalls Wilder, who was born nearby. I know all this because Z works at the Sun & Moon Art Gallery and at Little House Yoga and at Harmony Coffee on Laura Ingalls Wilder Avenue. Prophetstown is as different from Red Bend as a town can get and still be in Wisconsin.

The other thing Prophetstown has is music. All year long it has concerts and performances and festivals. Z loves this because she is a lifelong lover of anything musical, especially anything from the 1960s and 1970s, when all the best songs in the world were created, according to her. Other music-loving people live in Prophetstown too, including a man with a long gray ponytail who used to play with famous musicians in California. He and Z are friends, and so he has offered Paul music lessons. *For free.* Which is an enormously large deal because lessons are expensive and money does not grow in cans (that is a family joke). Paul is also into music, and all day long he is either practicing or listening. When he is doing his music, he is so focused that he cannot even hear people calling his name. We say he is on Planet Paul.

I have to go set the table because *Z is coming!* I cannot wait to show her this journal and tell her our plan. This summer could not get any better!

Thursday, June 13 — LATER

OMG. OMG. OMG. OMG. OMG. OMG. And I normally do not say those letters, even though when I say OMG, I mean "oh my gosh" and not "oh my the-other-one."

Remember how Z sent me this journal to write about my marvelous adventures and experiences-to-come? Well, now I know what she was talking about.

OMG.

Okay, I will *slow down a little* as Dad says sometimes when I am talking, and I will try to explain what happened.

Z came to supper tonight. Z coming to supper is an adventure in and of itself because she calls everyone darling and brings crazy not-at-all-like-a-grandmother gifts like a dead branch she thinks is beautiful or a book of nude portraits (!) or earrings she made herself that she said she'd pierce my ears with in a special ceremony. Z is always on a special diet such as eating only one color food each day of the week. Or only eating food that is raw. She has been every kind of vegetarian, including the kind that doesn't even eat honey. Sometimes she brings us organic potato chips or organic chocolate-covered peanuts. You'd think "organic" would mean "healthy," but that's not necessarily true in Z's case.

Lately Z does not eat anything made with wheat. She says the hardest part was giving up Oreos, but they are made with wheat flour, so even though they are absolutely delicious and perfect, they're out. If I ever stopped eating wheat, I would make a rule that I could only be 99% wheatless. The last 1% I would leave for Oreos.

Mom reads all the labels extra closely but she still usually gets something wrong. She has a glass of wine ready whenever Z comes, just in case. Wine for herself.

"Hello, darlings!" Z said when she arrived tonight. She gave us hugs that she says fill the universe with good karma and told Dad again that he is saving the world. Dad is an engineer in a factory that cans beans and corn and potatoes. During summer harvest, he works every day, seven days a week, because that's how fast the crops come in. Right now he's making sure the machines work, because beans start soon and then all canning heck will break loose.

Z picked up the wheat-free cookbook. "Oh, aren't you wonderful! . . . Did I forget to tell you that I'm back with wheat?"

There was a bit of a silence. Mom smiled brightly and reached for her wine.

Now Z can eat Oreos again!

At dinner, Z told her favorite story about dancing in St. Peter's Square in Rome. I've heard the story one hundred times (almost literally), but I still love it.

When Z was in college, she went to Italy on an art-studying trip, and while she was in Rome she visited a famous church called St. Peter's that has an open space in front with huge rows of columns like two arms. They built the columns on purpose to make the church look like it was hugging the whole world. Z has a drawing of St. Peter's Square hanging in her bedroom, and trust me, the hug feeling is extremely clear. It is called a square even though it is hug shaped.

When Z saw St. Peter's Square in real life, back when she was in college, she got so excited that she held out her arms to match the shape of the column hugs, and without warning an old Italian man came up and started dancing with her. Z's friends were totally shocked. Z just laughed, though, and went along with the old man, twirling around the square. The only words she could understand him saying were *bellissima* and *amore*. *Bellissima* means "very beautiful" and *amore* means "love." Then they finished and he bowed to her and that was it. The whole thing took less than a minute. That's why Z bought the drawing of St. Peter's Square — so she can always remember.

When I was little, I'd imagine Z as one of the little figures in the drawing, even though the drawing is from hundreds of years ago. Z would tell me the story, and then she'd hold out her arms and have me dance with her. The only problem was that I was terrible at dancing. We'd always fall down laughing on her bed. Maybe that's why I like the story so much, because it always reminds me of giggling with Z.

Anyway, Z told the story again tonight and we all laughed, and then Z laid down her fork. "I . . . I need to do it again."

Mom and Dad shared a glance.

"Dance with an old man?" Paul asked.

"That trip to Rome . . . it was a pilgrimage, you know."

Mom made a little sound under her breath.

"It was!" Z said. "It was not — I admit — a religious pilgrimage, but I was following in the footsteps of thousands of years of pilgrims. I intended to visit all seven pilgrimage churches, and I failed."

Z has told me this story too. Rome has seven churches that are particularly important, and when Z was my age she read a book about pilgrims visiting those seven churches, so when she was in Rome, she tried to do it too. But she ran out of time. She only made it to six of them. This isn't like the dancing-in-St.-Peter's-Square story. This story makes Z sad. She doesn't tell it much.

"I'm going to do it right this time," Z said. "I'm turning sixty-four this summer. I would like to reconnect with God."

Mom cleared her throat. "You know, Z, I'm pretty sure God is everywhere. You could probably connect with God in our living room."

Dad chuckled, but Z waved this away. "God has been in Rome for two thousand years. We'll have a better conversation there, God and me. I need to apologize."

"For the pilgrimage?" I asked. I've always felt bad about how Z never made it to that seventh church. It feels like a jigsaw puzzle with one piece missing. A corner piece.

Z nodded, kind of.

"Well," Dad said at last. "It sounds like a great trip — "

"There's one other thing," Z said. "I'd like to take Sarah with me."

BOOM. (That is the sound of all heck breaking loose. Although it broke quietly at first.)

Everyone stared at Z.

Then they stared at me.

Then we stared at Mom and Dad.

We even looked at Paul.

Mom cleared her throat again. "Now just a second. Your trip — that's fine. Do what you want. But this is a foreign country we're talking about. Sarah's only fourteen. I'm not sure you're the best . . . chaperone . . ." Mom shot Dad a look.

So Dad asked what Z was thinking timewise, and Z said we'd be leaving July 10 and returning July 17.

"You've already bought the tickets?" Mom asked in a coolish voice.

"The price was right. And — just so you know — they're nonrefundable. Not that it matters . . ."

BOOM.

Mom stared at her plate. I don't know what Dad and Z were doing because I was so busy watching Mom. I do know that Paul was gone, though. I hadn't even noticed him leaving.

Finally Dad said this sure was interesting and we all needed some time and he knew it'd work out in the end. Mom, on the other hand, said for me to go to my room.

So here I am.

Rome.

ROME!

Rome is such a famous and important city — it's the capital of Italy and head of the Catholic Church of the world. I would get to see those seven churches and St. Peter's Square (although I do not want anyone dancing with me!). I would get to be a *pilgrim* — not the Thanksgiving kind but the super-old-fashioned kind like the ones in Z's drawing. I would be part of history.

So those are pluses. But Mom is right too. Rome is in a foreign country on the other side of the globe. They don't speak English, and who knows what we would eat. I know the Italians invented pizza, but that doesn't mean that Italian pizza is any good; a lot of pizza isn't. Z says Italian ice cream is deliciously wonderful, but I am suspicious. I do not like most American ice cream flavors. And what if the plane crashes? Rome is thousands and thousands of miles away. That's a lot of miles to crash in. And what if someone tries to dance with me? I do not know how to say, *I'm a terrible dancer* in Italian. I do not know how to say, *But you could dance with my grandmother because she loves adventures.* I'm not sure people even say that in Italian.

I am extremely worried about everything I have just listed plus all the other terrible things I do not even know to list yet. But I'm most worried about Curtis. Because all the things I listed are things Curtis will worry about too. He will worry about them ten times more than me. He will worry $10x^2$ (= ten times squared).

Friday, June 14

Dad and Mom left for work before I got up, which I appreciate because I do not feel like talking about Rome. It is overwhelming even to think about. Instead I went to Curtis's baseball game. That, I decided, would be my Sarah Zorn adventure for the 14th of June. Red Bend baseball is as far from Rome-thinking as you can get.

Curtis is excellent at baseball. He is a utility player, which means he can play many different positions, including pitcher so long as there is not too much pressure. It is difficult to pitch under pressure, even for professionals, which is why pitchers are so well paid. He also plays third base and sometimes center field.

I like riding my bike to the park and sitting on the bleachers with the parents and the other baseball fans. The problem is that I do not like going to his games for other reasons. For one thing, it is often hot — so hot that some of the grownups use umbrellas, which I cannot do because Emily makes fun of me enough as it is. Instead

I wear an old fishing hat from one of Z's ex-boyfriends, which I know looks silly, but if I wear a baseball cap, my ears burn and I end up with hat head. Emily never seems to get hat head.

Emily is the other reason I don't like baseball. Emily attends all the games, with big posters that read GO RED BEND! GO CURTIS! She also cheers, which I do not do, because unlike some people, I am not naturally loud.

Sure enough, Emily was there with her friends, who were all cheering loudly. She came right over, even though I specifically sat on another bleacher, and asked if I had made a poster. Which I clearly had not because a poster is exceedingly visible, and also exceedingly difficult to carry on a bike. She asked why I never make posters. "If I was Curtis's girlfriend, I'd make a new poster for every game," Emily said. "I'd cheer for him a lot. And I'd be very loud so he could hear me."

I cannot imagine Emily cheering any louder than she already does.

"You know," Emily said, "I've had boyfriends. I know how to be a girlfriend, if you want some tips." Then she gave me her *I'm onto you* look and went back to her friends . . .

Okay. This is my personal private journal, so I will tell the truth. The truth about Curtis and me and our Brilliant Outflanking Strategy.

It started back in seventh grade with the hydrogen display that Curtis and I did for science class. The project itself was amazingly fun, but the other kids were awful. They kept teasing us and saying we were working on the project because we were boyfriend and girlfriend, which was especially bad because it was not true! We were only friends. We were good science friends, which is the best kind of friends to be.

We were teased so much that we would not even look at each other or do homework together after school. Last summer I did not see him at all.

Then, at the end of the summer, we both went to his sister's first football game and we talked a little. Then we both went to the Jorgensens' Labor Day picnic because our families go every year. Curtis told me about a possum skull he had just cleaned (Curtis collects skulls), and it felt exactly like old hydrogen times. Several little kids kept hanging around us because little kids love Curtis, and one girl (a future Emily, I think) kept asking if we were going out. I kept saying no, but she kept asking in a pestering way.

Finally I was so fed up that I said, "Yep, we are."

"I knew it," she said. And, zip, she ran off.

"Why did you say that?" Curtis looked horrified. He looked as horrified as I felt. We watched the little girl run up to a group of kids and elbow her way into the middle like she had something to say — to say about *us*. But instead she pointed to her T-shirt. She didn't even look back at Curtis and me. She was only talking about her clothes. She looked like she had already forgotten about us.

Curtis frowned. "Why would she keep asking us that question if she doesn't care?"

"She did care," I said, thinking hard. "Until we said yes. Then she stopped thinking about it." That was when I had my eureka moment. *Eureka* is what you say when you have a massive scientific discovery. "That's it! Curtis, no one cares if we're *really* going out. They just like thinking we are. They don't like it when we say they're wrong. So let's let them think it!"

Curtis looked at me like I was crazy, but in the end he agreed to try because neither of us could think of any better way to keep talking to each other without people teasing us.

The next day — the first day of eighth grade — we got to school and immediately started talking in the hall. Within one minute Brett Ortlieb said, "Oooh, you two are going out."

Normally I would say, *No!* But this time (*Please, Sarah, be right about this!*) I said, "Yep."

Brett Ortlieb looked confused. "Wait. You two are really going out?"

I nodded. Curtis stared at the floor, but that is not unusual for him.

Brett said, "Oh . . . ," and walked away. That was it.

That day, Curtis and I ate lunch together and walked home together and even worked on science together. No one said a single teasing thing. They just let us be.

This is why we call it the Brilliant Outflanking Strategy, because that is how brilliant it turned out to be. My parents think Curtis and I are going out — they give me lectures about it, which is how I can tell — and Paul does, and our friends and Curtis's parents and his sister, D.J., who has a boyfriend and gets a kick out of the fact that her little brother and I are boyfriend and girlfriend too, just like Brian and her. Although Curtis is not a quarterback like Brian is. Or eighteen years old. Or going to college.

Emily is the only person who is suspicious. No one else expects us to kiss in public or hug all the time, because they know we are not like that. But not Emily. Whenever Curtis and I are together, she watches us as though she is preparing her own science-fair project. I do not like it at all.

Emily is probably suspicious because around boys she is the exact opposite of me. She is always laughing at boys' dumb stories and giggling when they touch her gluteus maximus, and she makes out in the halls. Even

though I tell myself I am not like Emily, I worry sometimes that sitting in the bleachers watching Curtis play
baseball makes me look like her. I do not want anyone
thinking that ever.

I have not talked about this with Curtis. We are not
good at talking about anything related to Emily, and
also I do not think he would understand, because he is
(*duh*) a boy. Sometimes I get so worried about whether
I look like Emily that I leave his games early. But I tell
Curtis I have to be somewhere else, or that Mom or
Paul is calling me.

Anyway, that was an extremely long description of
Curtis and me and the Brilliant Outflanking Strategy.
Now we can return to today's baseball game and the
fact that I was doing my best not to think about Rome.

I stayed until the end of the game. Curtis's team
won — hurray. He was supposed to leave right away for
a weekend tournament in Sheboygan, but his mom said
he had time to get ice cream. That's something the two
of us do. It's nice because it's what boy/girlfriends do,
but it's what friend-friends do too.

"Hey," I said when he came up. "Nice game." We
Palm Saluted and smiled. Every time we Palm Salute, I
smile.

"Thanks. Boris says hello, by the way."

"Will he be okay while you're gone?" I was not

completely joking. I do not want anything happening to Boris. Being dead is bad enough.

Curtis said he'd double-checked and that Boris would be fine. We walked toward Jorgensens' Ice Cream. I asked Curtis what he thought about Emily's poster.

Curtis shrugged. "She sure cheers a lot."

That was not what I wanted to hear. I wanted him to say posters are stupid and he doesn't like Emily coming to his games and he doesn't like her, period. What did he mean, *she cheers a lot*? "Doesn't she cheer too much?"

"Nah . . . It's kind of crazy, you know, how she does it . . ."

I wanted to ask if Curtis wanted me to cheer, but it's the kind of thing Emily would ask, so I couldn't. I wouldn't ask that even if Curtis and I actually were going out.

We did not say much more after this, and we got our chocolate (Curtis) and vanilla (me) and sat under a tree and ate our cones. Sometimes we discuss trying other flavors, but that didn't seem like a good thing to talk about today. Nothing did.

I wanted to tell Curtis about Rome, but I did not know how to bring it up. It is interesting that Curtis and Z are my two favorite people in the world and yet they are total opposites. Z never thinks about what could go wrong, and Curtis only thinks about what could. Once he told me that he wished he could drive my school bus because then he'd know I'd be safe.

But I would have to tell him eventually, right? "Z wants to take a trip to Rome to be a pilgrim again, and she invited me to go with her."

Curtis frowned. "Rome, *Italy?*"

I nodded.

"Would you fly there?"

"Well, yeah. If I go."

"What if the plane crashes?"

See? He always worries. Why couldn't he say, *That sounds like fun?* I am also worried about crashing, but that is not reason enough not to go. "Flying isn't that dangerous."

"Rome is really far away," Curtis said.

"I know. But my grandmother would say that that's why you go."

Curtis ripped up a handful of grass. "That seems like a really bad reason to go somewhere."

"Well, I don't even know if I'm going yet." I was the one who should be nervous about traveling, not Curtis. Curtis goes everywhere. He goes to Sheboygan.

We ate our ice cream in silence. Then his mom pulled up and he left.

Monday, June 17

My weekend was not productive. I spent the whole time thinking about Curtis and Rome but I got nowhere with my thoughts.

This morning, D.J. drove Paul and me to Prophetstown.

Mom stayed home from work until D.J. got there to make sure we knew what we were doing et cetera. As soon as D.J. pulled up in front of our house, Paul took his guitar and headphones and climbed into the back seat of her car so he wouldn't have to sit next to her. Sitting next to her was obviously going to be my job.

We rode awhile without saying anything. I wondered if I should ask about Curtis and what he's thinking, which D.J. might know given that she's his sister. I didn't want to be the one to bring it up, though.

"So," D.J. asked, "you doing anything fun this summer besides walking dogs?" Oh: Curtis had not talked to her — but he had been in Sheboygan all weekend.

"My grandmother wants to take me to Rome. Rome, *Italy*."

"Cool . . . That is really, really cool. What are you going to do there?"

I said we were going to visit churches, and then D.J.

asked about Z, and so I spent the rest of the car ride describing her. Describing Z could take a whole car ride and then some.

Z is not a normal grandmother. Normal grandmothers don't wear four earrings in one ear and two in the other, or dress in loose, dangling clothes that make you look like a hippie, which is what Z used to be. She is the only grandmother I know who goes on water slides, and when she slides down she makes a noise like a cowboy. The other kids on the water slide were extremely impressed.

Z was born in Two Geese, Wisconsin, but then she moved to California and Oregon and New York City. She did not come back to Wisconsin until my great-grandmother Ann got sick — which I remember because I was five when Grandma Ann died — and then Z decided to stay. Now she lives in Prophetstown in an apartment in an old painted house with a dog named Jack Russell George.

I am in Z's apartment now, eating Oreos with milk and writing this down. It is important to eat Oreos the right way. Z and I are in agreement on this, and Paul, too. We are dunkers, not scrapers. Eating the filling first is a violation of everything that is the Oreo Way and also leaves you with two dry cookie halves. Not good. Luckily we live in the dairy state of

Wisconsin, so milk is readily available. Z used to tease me that *milk* was *Oreo* spelled backwards. She jokes that that's how I learned to read so early — from reading all those Oreos. She says Oreos + yoga keep her young.

Now I am going to walk Jack Russell George.

Monday, June 17 — LATER

Training a dog is a lot harder than it looks.

Jack Russell George is extremely smart, even for a Jack Russell terrier. This is how smart he is: when Z is at work and he has no one to play with, he drops a tennis ball down the stairs and runs down and catches it at the bottom and does it again. This is hilarious to watch and I am sure it is excellent exercise, but it is also noisy. The sculptor who lives upstairs from Z does not find it hilarious at all. That is where I come in. I am supposed to walk Jack Russell George to the park and throw him a tennis ball so he can release all his stair-bouncing kilowatts of energy.

The problem is that while Jack Russell George is tremendously good at fetching the ball, he is not so interested in returning it.

I think I need a book on dogs.

I am back home in Red Bend now. On the ride back, Paul listened to music in the back seat and ignored us. I asked D.J. about her basketball practice. She said it went really well and she really likes playing with girls on this level. But she was far more interested in Z than in basketball, which I appreciated because then I could contribute to the conversation. D.J. wanted to know, for example, why we call her Z, which is a tremendously long story and it makes some people uncomfortable, so I have to be careful how I tell it.

You see, Z had Dad when she was only eighteen years old. My dad was born in the 1960s, when a lot of people didn't like girls having babies when they weren't married, and Z had to drop out of college and move back to Two Geese. But Z didn't want to stay in northern Wisconsin with a baby, and she couldn't raise him on her own, so she kind of gave Dad to her parents and then moved to California, where there was more work and stuff for someone like her. Dad grew up in Two Geese with a bunch of uncles and aunts, including an uncle who is only three years older than he is. Uncle Tommy's more like an older brother. And out in California my grandmother changed her name from Alice Zorn to Azalea Zorn, but everyone called her Z. Even my dad as a little kid said Z because he already called his grandmother Mom. Sometimes Z jokes that she's Plan Z, as in the opposite of Plan A. She's the last resort.

"Plan Z . . ." D.J. laughed. "I like that." Then she asked the question people usually ask. "So, who's — if you're okay talking about it — who's your dad's dad?"

I chewed on a hangnail, but then I stopped because that is bad for your nails. "Z was in New York, you know, when it happened, and she's really, really into music, and Dad's full name is Robert Zimmerman Zorn . . ."

D.J. looked blank. A lot of people do not know who that is.

"Robert Zimmerman is the real name of Bob Dylan. You know, that singer from the 1960s? He wrote 'Like a Rolling Stone' and a bunch of other songs . . ."

"Your grandfather is Bob Dylan?"

"No. Z says he's not. She's never said who Dad's father is. She named Dad that because Bob Dylan was born in a small town in Minnesota and he ended up world famous, and she wanted her son to know he didn't have to be in a small town forever. Also she really likes Bob Dylan."

"So Z wanted your father to be famous?"

"She wanted him . . . she wanted him to know he had options."

"Huh," said D.J., thinking about this. "That's wild."

"Do you know what I think?" I lowered my voice. "I think my dad's father *is* someone famous — someone famous besides Bob Dylan. Z knew a lot of famous people — you should see her apartment. She's always saying a girl has to watch herself around musicians. I think that's why she taught Paul music — so he'd have some luck with girls."

We both looked back at Paul with his eyes closed, jamming on his air guitar.

"Huh," D.J. said again. She did not say, *That seems like a stretch*, although I bet that's what she was thinking. I was thinking it.

"Z loves coming to your basketball games," I told D.J., which is a true fact and I have been waiting for a good time to tell her and this seemed like it. "She is your hugest fan."

D.J. laughed. "Whew, now I know . . . Thanks for the chat." Because by then we were home.

Riding with D.J. Schwenk is a lot easier than I'd thought it would be.

Thursday, June 20

I have been supremely busy reading *Two Lady Pilgrims in Rome*. It is a book that Z mailed to me with a note saying "I hope you love this old sourpuss as much as I do!" It was written more than a hundred and fifty years ago by a lady named Miss Lillian Hesselgrave who went to Rome with a friend and visited all seven pilgrimage churches. That's why Z went on her pilgrimage, to copy Miss Hesselgrave.

Z is right. Miss Hesselgrave is absolutely a sourpuss. She complains about everything: indecent ladies and Roman drivers and bad Roman tea. She describes a church as being beautiful and mysterious with incense and chanting priests and pilgrims in brown cloaks, so I can 100% understand why Z would want to go there . . . but then in the next sentence she warns about the deadly night air! It is like she is saying, *You must visit Rome, but for goodness' sake don't go there!* I am not sure why this was one of Z's favorite books. Perhaps there wasn't a lot to read in Two Geese, Wisconsin.

I will tell you what is interesting, though: trying to figure out what Miss Hesselgrave is talking about. For example, when she says Rome ladies are indecent, she doesn't mean indecent like the way Emily dresses. She means that they show their ankles. When she complains about Roman drivers, she means horse drivers because there weren't any cars back then. And I think that when she talks about bad night air, she means air pollution ... although you'd think the air would be polluted during the day too — polluted from all those horses.

I hope the Romans have fixed their air since then, because if — IF — I go, I do not want to have to worry about air pollution.

Today I went to another baseball game and you-know-who was there. Curtis didn't look much at her, but he didn't look much at me, either. He focused on the game.

I left before it ended.

Friday, June 21

Today D.J. asked Paul if he was going to Rome too.

Paul looked surprised. "I'm playing this summer," he said, like that explained everything. "The guitar."

"Oh," D.J. said. You could tell she was trying not to smile. "That's cool."

"Yeah ..." he said, already on Planet Paul.

So D.J. talked to me instead. She doesn't seem to mind that I'm three years younger than she is. I appreciate that. I like that D.J. will be at Red Bend High School in the fall. It means I will know a senior who will also know me. I also appreciate that D.J. is not the kind of girl who mentions her boyfriend every two minutes like some girls I can think of (= Emily Enemy).

D.J. had so many questions about Z that when we got to Prophetstown I invited her up to Z's apartment, because Z's apartment is unique and special. One entire end of Z's living room is record albums — the big old-fashioned kind. Hundreds of them. And all over the walls are photographs of Z with bands and with other famous people, or at places like Woodstock, which was a famous music recital back in the 1960s.

"Whoa," D.J. breathed. She studied the pictures. "Do you know who these people are?"

"No, but Z does." (*Duh, Sarah.*) "I know the albums, though. I used to study the covers for hours."

"Look at this guy! It looks like a ferret climbed onto his face and died."

"People used to be exceedingly good at hair," I said.

"I'll say. Keep these dudes away from open flame . . . Shoot, I've got to go. But this place is great. I wish I knew someone like this."

Then she left and I walked Jack Russell George and wrote in this journal and tried not to eat all of Z's Oreos. D.J. had some of Z's Oreos too, before she left. D.J. is also a dunker. She is even cooler now that I know that.

Z likes D.J., and now D.J. Schwenk likes my grandmother too. The universe feels extremely happy right now.

Friday, June 21 — LATER

D.J. did talk about her boyfriend today on the ride back to Red Bend, but it wasn't in an Emily-bragging kind of way. She said that this weekend they're going to Lake Superior with Brian's parents and her mom is freaking about it. But, she says, her mom shouldn't worry, because Brian's mother is as strict as she needs to be. I did not ask her what that meant specifically.

I do not know what D.J. would think of Curtis's and my Brilliant Outflanking Strategy. But I suspect someone who has a real boyfriend would not approve of someone who has a fake one, particularly if that fake boyfriend is her brother.

D.J. asked if we'd decided about Rome. I said no and that there was still a lot to figure out.

"I bet." D.J. nodded in a sympathetic kind of way.

Mom was home when we got back to Red Bend, and she invited D.J. in so she could pay her. She offered D.J. a pop, but D.J. said she just wanted to get home and shower.

"What do you think of this whole Rome business?"

Mom asked D.J., rummaging around in her purse for money.

D.J. leaned against the door frame. "The trip, you mean? Sounds like a pretty great learning experience." She grinned at me. "I bet even Sarah could be smarter."

Then D.J. left and Mom started supper. She didn't start right away, though. She stood there for a long time staring at the counter.

Saturday, June 22

Z came for supper tonight and brought Chinese food. At least this time the vegetables weren't all purple. That happened once when she was on her one-color-a-day diet, and it was not good.

Z also brought a sample poster for the Dog Days of Prophetstown, which is a huge festival that Prophetstown will be holding in August with a dog talent show and a dog parade and dog portraitists (of dogs, not by dogs), and Z is going to lead an outdoor yoga class called Downward Dog — which is a real yoga position — for dogs and people both.

"Do dogs even do yoga?" Mom asked.

"We'll find out, won't we?" Z said with a bark (ha! joke!) of laughter.

Z brought us fortune cookies, too. I find fortune

cookies fascinating even though they do not actually predict the future. Here is what our cookies said:

1. Paul: *Be alert to good news.* Paul said he would try.
2. Mom: *Today exists between yesterday and tomorrow.* Mom said, "Thank goodness someone finally clarified that for me." Mom does not appreciate fortune cookies.
3. Dad: *You will solve a problem.* Dad always solves problems; it's his job. Not so insightful, that cookie.
4. Sarah (= me): *That which is priceless has no cost.* Mom rolled her eyes, but I was okay with it.
5. Z: *Hell is paved with good intentions.*

Z frowned when she read it, and I noticed Mom and Dad looked at each other. But then Z grabbed a pen and carefully added the words *Heaven is paved with Oreos.* She held it up. "Much better, don't you think?"

We all agreed it was.

If you look at the beginning of this journal, you can see I have taped *Heaven is paved with Oreos* on the cover. And I'll tell you one thing: Z's heaven will definitely have Oreos in it.

Z is still here, talking in the kitchen with Mom and Dad. I suppose I should be there too, consider-

ing they're probably talking about Rome (which, by
the way, no one mentioned at supper, which means
something). But then they'll ask me what I think,
and *I DO NOT KNOW*. Z says I should go, Curtis says I shouldn't, Miss Hesselgrave says . . . I
don't know what she would say, but it is definitely
something disapproving. D.J. says it could make me
smarter . . .

I like the idea of Rome making me smarter. I will
admit that I like that idea a lot.

Sunday, June 23

Mom and Dad said — well, they didn't say I could go to
Rome. They said it was my decision but that they were
okay with my going. I heard this and I thought, *Thanks
a lot, guys — I have no idea!*

But then I realized I actually did have an idea. I want
to see all the things that Miss Hesselgrave talks about. I
want to be smart for high school. I want to be a worldly
world traveler.

So . . .

I AM GOING TO ROME.

I called Z to tell her, and she said she knew all the
time that I would do it.

I think Mom and Dad like the idea of me getting smarter too.

Sunday, June 23 — LATER

I called Curtis.

When I wish him a good game, do I sound that bad? Because when he said "Have a good trip," it did not sound good at all.

Monday, June 24

I told D.J. about my Rome decision. She did not indicate in any way that she had already heard the news from Curtis. Instead she said, "Fantastic! Send me a postcard of your favorite place. So you'll have to visit a lot of places."

"Hey," Paul said from the back seat. "You know what? We should have a birthday party for Z when you guys get back. I can play her favorite song. She's going to be sixty-four, you know."

"Is 'When I'm Sixty-Four' her favorite song?" D.J. asked.

"Nah. But she taught me that one too. *If I am old*

and balding and gray in the years to come, would you like me, think of me as honey dear? Buy me biscuits? Bring me a beer?"

D.J. laughed. "That is not how the song goes!"

"Beatles lyrics are, like, impossible to get permission to, so Z and I made up our own. *If I go out and drink with my friends, will you pace the floor? Could you adore me? Please don't abhor me, when I'm sixty-four."*

I couldn't believe it. Paul barely *says* this many words in a week — let alone singing them! His lessons must be going really well. And D.J. is psyched about her basketballing club. That means ⅔ of the people in D.J.'s car are in extremely good moods, which makes the last ⅓ person (= me) feel even worse.

Why did Curtis have to say "Have a good trip" like that? Because even though the words were "Have a good trip," they sounded like *I'm not happy at all.*

Tuesday, June 25

Curtis had a game today. I asked if he wanted me to come, and he said it was up to me. He used to say he liked it when I came. So should I go or not? (Even asking the question is Emily-ish of me.) I wish there was someone I could talk to about this. Not Curtis, obviously. Not D.J. — Curtis is not a subject I could ever bring up! I can't talk to Z.

You would not think so, but Z is actually a difficult person to talk to about personal things. Last year when I got my period for the first time, I called to tell her, and that night she came to supper with a cake with WELCOME TO WOMANHOOD! written on it in pink frosting letters. Sometimes Z says I will do well in life because I have excellent judgment in men (her words). But then she'll say I must be relentlessly alert to male oppression and that I need to experience the universe unfettered.

Last year Dad had a conference in Canada and Z went with us — that's when we went on the water slide, and I had to get a passport (for Canada, not the water slide). On the way back we drove through Two Geese, her old town. All of a sudden Z's happy mood changed and she wouldn't even let Dad stop the car. She just kept staring out the window and saying, "This is a terrible place to grow up."

"Z, it's not 1960 anymore," Dad said. But I don't think she heard him. She couldn't understand that the time is different and the place is different and the people are different too.

That's why, even though I can talk to Z about proper Oreo technique and dancing in St. Peter's Square, I can't tell her about my baseball confusion or the Brilliant

Outflanking Strategy. Because sometimes she can't always see me as me, but only me as her. And if I did tell her about the Brilliant Outflanking Strategy, she would probably write it in pink letters on a cake.

Friday, June 28

I would appreciate it if D.J. brought up Curtis once in a while. If you were riding with us and did not know the Schwenk family, you would not know she even has brothers. That is how little she mentions them.

"By the way, how was your weekend at Lake Superior?" I asked to make conversation.

"It was great. It was . . . great. But you know, boyfriends are hard."

"Yes, they are," I said. I did not add *Even when they're fake they're hard.* I was silent for that.

Saturday, June 29

Today Mom and I went shopping for the trip. Mom wants me to get comfortable shoes so I can walk a lot, and I want to get shoes that do not make me look eighty years old. The shoes Mom likes make me look older than Z. Z's shoes are actually cool looking most of the time, especially for a grandmother. They are hip yoga-lady shoes.

Mom held up one pair, and I said, "Z would never wear those."

"Z has bunions," Mom said. Completely missing my point. "And besides, aren't pilgrims supposed to be plain?"

I was trying to explain that "plain" does not mean "dorky" when guess who walked into the shoe store at that exact moment: Emily. Of course.

"Oooh," she said, "those shoes are so you!"

"See?" Mom said. Again: completely missing the point.

"So what are you and Curtis up to tonight?" Emily asked with an expression of extraordinarily false innocence as Mom went searching for more old-lady shoes.

"He's coming over to play chess." This is true. We set it up yesterday.

"Very exciting!" Emily leaned in closer. "What else are you going to do?"

"Nothing," I said. I tried to sound icy.

Emily smiled knowingly. "I didn't think so . . . Oh, I've got to go. Bye, Mrs. Zorn. Very nice to see you."

It will not surprise you that Mom then said how nice Emily was and did not notice how I was mad. Then she bought a pair of shoes for me that I hate. I hope I don't see anyone in Rome I know.

Saturday, June 29 — LATER

Curtis just left my house. We did not have fun. I could not stop thinking about Emily and how she asked if there was anything else we were doing. That is none of her business!

1. It is our relationship, and we can do whatever we like.
2. We are not actually going out, and therefore we should not be doing anything else even if we wanted to.
3. If we did want to do something else (which we do not), we could not do it in my house because of how much trouble we got in last fall during our desiccation science-fair project when Curtis and I stayed up all night working in our basement building Plexiglas containers to display dried rats in. Mom and Dad freaked about Curtis staying over because they thought we were doing something else, and Curtis's parents freaked too. And even though everyone now knows about the science fair, Curtis is not allowed in our basement anymore.
4. Speaking of science fairs, we have a calf to as-

semble. That is a good something else to be doing!

So that was one reason we didn't have fun, because I was so busy thinking those thoughts. But it was worse even than that, because it turns out that not only did Emily say that mean thing to me this afternoon, but a friend of hers also asked Curtis to the movies. He said no.

"Did you want to go?" I asked.

He shrugged. "Did you?"

"They didn't invite me." I could not believe I had to explain this.

"Yeah . . . I didn't know what to say."

You could say that they shouldn't invite you without inviting me, I thought. Instead I said, "That would be hard, I guess."

"Yeah. Because explaining everything . . . us, you know. It's not . . . easy."

"Oh," I said. We kept playing. But I wasn't paying attention anymore. I didn't even care when he took both my rooks. Normally I care a lot.

"I'm sleeping over at Peter's tonight," Curtis said after a while.

"Oh. Okay."

"You know, his mom and stuff . . . I don't want to be late . . ."

It was not late, but he left anyway. I didn't know what to say. I still don't.

Monday, July 1

D.J. had two basketball games today. On the way to Prophetstown she didn't talk at all because she was so nervous.

I walked Jack Russell George same as always (we now play actual fetch instead of just catch-and-run-away!) and guess who was in Z's apartment when we got back: Z! She was sitting at her kitchen table with a box of colored markers. "What do you think?" she asked, holding up a Dog Days of Prophetstown poster. On the back she had written I SAY D.J.! in big bubble letters.

You would not think of my grandmother as a crazy sports fan, but you would be wrong. Z is actually quite a fan in her yoga hippie kind of way. She has been watching D.J. Schwenk play basketball for years — even before Curtis and I became friends. She says her Wisconsin heritage left her with a love of milk and a love of basketball. Especially girls' basketball. Especially good girls' basketball.

"Don't you have a sign made?" Z asked. "Oh, never

mind, we're late already. Come on, darling! We need to envelop the court with our karma!"

I am glad I do not play basketball against D.J. Schwenk. Yes, this morning D.J. was so nervous in the car that she could not talk. But walking out from the locker room, she hid her nervousness extremely well. On the court she looked even more like a lion than she normally does. She looked like she had picked out one player for dinner and another one for dessert.

We had an amazingly good time, Z and I. Z waved her I SAY D.J.! sign, and she kept asking the man in front of us why the umpire was blowing his whistle. I think she was flirting. It was nice to see other people in the stands cheering for D.J. too. D.J. has a lot more fans than she realizes, I think. I was proud to know her. And Z was tickled that D.J. had visited her apartment and liked it so much. "That girl ate my Oreos!" Z said to the man in front of us. Somehow it did not sound crazy when she said it. It just made us laugh.

I had a question for Z, though, and during halftime I worked up the courage to ask it: "How bad is the air in Rome?" I cannot stop worrying about this. Seriously: Miss Hesselgrave talks about bad Roman air all the time.

"Oh, darling!" Z laughed. "I should have told you!" It turns out Rome actually did used to have *bad air* — or, as they say in Italian, *mal'aria* — but the real problem was mosquitoes. Mosquitoes flew around at night and bit people and made them sick with malaria, only at the time no one figured out it was the bugs. They all just thought it was the air. Isn't that fascinating? I feel so much better now.

I wish I could tell Curtis about Roman malaria and paranoid Miss Hesselgrave and how even she didn't figure out it was mosquitoes. He would find it fascinating too. But he and I have not communicated since last week. I think something is wrong.

Saturday, July 6

Curtis and I have broken up. I know: how can we break up when we were never going out? But we did.

It started because he came over to get ice cream. We didn't say much. We just walked over to Jorgensens' for our chocolate and vanilla. We didn't even talk about Boris. I wanted to talk about the malaria bad-air business, but it didn't seem like the right time.

"I don't like what we do," he said finally.

"What do you mean? Boris? Chess? Ice cream?"

"I don't like having a fake girlfriend."

"Oh." I did not know what else to say. *What about our Brilliant Outflanking Strategy?*

Curtis stared at the ground. "I want a real girl-friend." He would not even look at me.

"Oh," I said again. "Emily."

There was a long silence. "No . . . but Emily doesn't lie to people. I like that."

We sat there for a long time not saying anything. I no longer had any interest in my vanilla.

"We're not lying," I said finally; "we're outflanking. What's wrong with that?"

"Everything," Curtis said. "And if you don't see that, maybe we shouldn't be doing this anymore. This whole . . . thing."

I was shocked. "But what about Boris?"

Curtis shook his head. "I don't feel much like Boris at the moment."

I thought about pointing out that this was good because Boris is dead. But it would be a terrible joke. Also at that moment I felt exactly like Boris. Except Boris never had to break up with someone. And Boris never had to go to high school.

Tuesday, July 9

I am all packed. Tomorrow we go to Minneapolis, then Chicago, then Rome.

I told Z about breaking up with Curtis. I couldn't help it. That was how I phrased it too: "We broke up." Not *We stopped fake-going-out with our Brilliant Outflanking Strategy.*

Z sighed and said she wasn't surprised. "Sometimes there's just not a spark."

I tried to agree with her, but I may have been crying. Even fake relationships can hurt, no matter how much sparking there might not be.

"Listen, darling," she said. "Forget about boys. Tomorrow we begin an enormous adventure. We are going to the Eternal City! We're going to be two girls on the town!"

"Just like Miss Hesselgrave and her companion," I said. Trying to cheer myself up.

"Well, yes . . . But I will not wear a corset. Do you hear me?"

That made me smile, the image of Z with a corset.

"We are pilgrims — pilgrims of adventure! We are adventurers to the great beyond!"

Z is exactly right. I have the rest of my life for men — I don't need them gumming things up now. I will go to Rome. I will show Curtis I don't need a fake boyfriend to have a real life.

JOURNAL #2

Wednesday, July 10

Z and I are on the plane to Chicago! We have an exceedingly tight connection to the plane to Rome — we may have to run!

Did you notice that I'm writing in a new journal? I don't think Z would find the cover of this journal quite as "glorious." But the old journal was already half-filled, and I did not want to run out of space, especially on my first *real* adventure. Also I do not want to carry around memories of Curtis. I can remember him without a book. I don't want to remember these last few weeks anyway. I have put that journal away so that someday I can read it again. Someday that is not anytime close to today.

Mom and Paul drove Z and me to the airport. Mom cried when we said goodbye, but I didn't. Paul waved, but I do not believe he will even notice I'm gone. He will only notice when he has to ride alone with D.J. Even then I think he will still be on Planet Paul.

Curtis did not wave because he was not there. Obviously. He did not say goodbye. I had not meant to point all this out, but I cannot help it. I do not think saying goodbye is what an ex–fake boyfriend is expected to do, but I think a real friend-friend is.

We are about to land. I have to put this away before the flight attendant says something to me.

Wednesday, July 10 — LATER

We didn't miss our flight to Rome! I think we were the last people to board — the man next to Z had already spread his stuff out onto her seat. He was not pleased when she showed up.

Z and I are not sitting together. I guess the tickets she bought were the right price because they're in different rows. But I can still hear her laugh. I think she made up with the man next to her. I, on the other hand, am sitting next to a nun — a real nun! Who is dressed in black with a headdress! I feel like I'm already in Rome! I think she is from another country, because she was reading a magazine in a different language — I think maybe Spanish. It didn't have any pictures in it. Also her English is not terribly good.

The nun had a glass of wine with supper. I think it is okay for nuns to drink wine, though really it is none of my business. My supper was lasagna and a salad and a roll and a tiny chocolate cake, and it was extremely good. Far better than what the cafeteria serves and better than what Mom usually makes, although I will not tell Mom that. I got pop, too, which I never get with supper, but I am on vacation.

Z and the man next to her got wine more than once.

It is important that I sleep because we will be landing at two o'clock in the morning our time, although it will be normal morning time for the Italians. Even the nun is taking out her little travel pillow. I have said "good night," and she said "good night" and also "God bless you," which must have extra-special power when a nun says it. Kind of like Z reconnecting with God from Rome rather than our living room.

I will not say who it is I wish was next to me right now. But I will say the name of someone who I'm glad isn't: Emily. I bet Emily wouldn't be brave enough to do this trip.

I will not think about what Emily might be doing in Red Bend.

Wednesday, July 10 — LATER

I think I can hear Z snoring.

Thursday, July 11

WE ARE IN ROME!!!

We are sitting outside at a little table at a coffee shop that Italians call a *caffè*, which is pronounced "cah-fey," next to people who are smoking and speaking in a different language, and we are in Rome. We called Mom to tell her we landed safely, and she said she's pleased everything is going so well. Z did not want Mom and me to talk long. Z says we must drink in every moment, and communicating with Wisconsin will prevent us from doing that. I am glad she has that rule, because now, even though I think about Curtis, I don't have to worry about what he and I would say. I can't talk to him because I am drinking.

We landed at an airport and took a train from the airport into the center of Rome. The whole experience felt like a dream because it was sunny and morning, but my body kept telling me it was 2:00 a.m. Everything looks different, even the trees. They are either extremely tall and skinny like pencils, or wide like umbrellas — they look like something from Dr. Seuss. And guess what I saw: goats! A real herd of real goats, climbing on a little hill and nibbling at things. I am guessing they were nibbling; the train was going so fast that I didn't have time to tell for sure. But they implied nibbling.

Those goats made me smile. They made me feel like Rome has been here forever.

From the train station we walked to our hotel. You can usually pick out the tourists because they have shoes that look like Mom bought them. But sometimes you see a man in a suit who has shoes that are black and shiny, or a woman who is dressed up and wearing high heels even though the streets are bumpy cobblestones that would be dangerous to walk on in heels, not to mention impossible — and those people are Roman. That's what Z says, anyway. There are almost no dogs. I guess Italians don't like dogs. Jack Russell George would have lots to smell, but no one to wag to.

Our hotel room is tiny and dark and foreign. The bathtub is much smaller than a normal bathtub. A lot of people I know would not fit in this tub. None of the Schwenks would. They would have to fold in half just to rinse.

Z and I unpacked our clothes, which did not take long, and just as I was sitting down Z said, "We must not sit or we will never stand up again!" So off we went to explore the Eternal City (= Rome's nickname). We only went a little ways, though, before we sat down again, at this caffè. But a caffè is different from a hotel room. Even if you don't drink anything, you're still drinking in every moment!

So we are drinking coffee and drinking Rome. Z is having a cappuccino. She says Italian coffee is better than American coffee could ever be, and she works in a coffee shop! She even let me have a kind of cappuccino with lots of milk that came in a glass like it was juice — coffee juice! — and it was delicious once I added sugar.

Here are the Italian words that Z knows:

1. *Ciao* = hello or goodbye. You pronounce it "chaow," kind of like *meow* but only one syllable. Z says it all the time. I am not sure she uses it correctly.
2. *Grazie* = thank you. It's pronounced "grot-see-ay."

Z also knows words like *pasta* and *pizza* and *spaghetti* and *cappuccino*. And *caffè,* and the names of the churches. And the name of the hotel. And *bellissima* and *amore.* But she most definitely cannot say *My granddaughter and I are lost and could you please direct us to the nearest clean bathroom.* When Z said that she spoke Italian, it may have been wishful thinking.

Miss Hesselgrave did not know Italian either. She says not to bother because the Romans will always pretend not to understand. And she says a woman must never under any circumstances travel in Rome without a male escort. But she also says that two American ladies when properly protected are quite enough to navigate the city. By "protected" she means parasols and comfortable shoes. Z and I do not have parasols, but we do have comfortable shoes, so I think even without a male escort or Italian or parasols, we will be okay.

The sky is extremely sunny, but that is not a problem because I have my fisherman's hat and sunglasses, and I now have a great deal of energy, which is good because Z has just said that we must muster and prepare to walk!

Thursday, July 11 — LATER

Z and I came to Rome to be pilgrims, but we will start being pilgrims tomorrow. Today we are only tourists.

Rome used to have lots of pilgrims back in Miss Hesselgrave's olden days. You could tell they were pilgrims because they dressed in brown and carried wooden walking sticks and looked like they'd been walking for months, which some of them had, to visit Rome and especially the seven churches. Going to all seven churches helped you get into heaven. Pilgrims weren't supposed to have money either but instead rely on the kindness of strangers. If you were a really good pilgrim, you would walk to all seven churches in one day even though they're miles and miles apart.

Miss Hesselgrave made it clear in *Two Lady Pilgrims in Rome* that she was not *that* kind of pilgrim. She liked the walking part and she was a fan of God, but she stayed in hotels and never once relied on strangers' kindnesses. Miss Hesselgrave had a low opinion of strangers, especially Roman strangers. She also took several days to visit the seven churches, and she spent more time describing the artwork and the history than she did the religious part. I think she felt religion was too personal to put in a book. History and art she could talk about forever. Trust me.

Rome doesn't have any pilgrims now, though, at least not pilgrims who dress in brown and beg for food and look like they've walked for months. Well, it has some people who look like that, but I think they're homeless people. They don't look church oriented if you know what I mean.

I do not see anyone else carrying a copy of *Two Lady Pilgrims in Rome.* I do see lots of people carrying guidebooks and maps.

Right now it is late afternoon. We are sitting in another caffè, which is how I can write; I could not walk and write at the same time! I am eating my first *gelato*, which means "ice cream" although it doesn't taste like ice cream. I asked Z for vanilla, but she made a mistake and got something else. It is good, but it does not taste like home.

I do not miss Curtis at all. Not one little bit.

We have walked so far — our hotel was only the beginning. The first thing we visited was an old building called the Pantheon. It is an old Roman temple with columns in front that are huge — bigger than any columns

I have ever seen, even in Chicago and Canada and Minneapolis — and each column is made out of a single piece of stone! They each must weigh tons and tons and tons. The columns weren't lifted in place by machinery, either: they were put there by people. *Roman* as in *two thousand years ago.* It is amazing that the columns haven't fallen down yet. An important person is buried inside, because two soldiers stand in front of his tomb. The soldiers don't move, but they are real. You can tell. The ceiling has a hole in the middle for sunlight to come in, and pigeons fly through it.

Then Z took me to see an elephant. I was extremely disappointed at first, because I thought she meant a live elephant, which this was not. It is a statue. But it is possibly the cutest statue I have ever seen in my life, of a little baby elephant who is waving his trunk and smiling, and on his back he has an obelisk. An obelisk, if you don't know, is a stone thing that looks like the Washington monument, only smaller. They are all over Rome. Miss Hesselgrave says obelisks are an eternal expression of the Roman character. She does not sound approving when she says this.

There are postcard stands everywhere, but I will not write a postcard to Curtis. You do not write to someone you've broken up with, no matter how much you think about him, *which I am not.* But if I did write him, this is what the postcard would say:

Dear Curtis:

We are here in Rome. It is hot. How is Boris? I have not seen any cows, though I did see goats. I hope baseball is going well. I wish I could show you the elephant.

Ciao, Sarah.

Now Z says we have to walk more. I wish I could dunk my feet in gelato.

Thursday, July 11 — LATER

I cannot believe Miss Hesselgrave does not complain about her feet — she is tougher than I realized, no matter how much she criticizes Roman air and Roman drivers.

After the Pantheon, Z and I walked to the really old part of Rome — the Forum — which is a bunch of rocks and tourists and (you can smell) cats. We watched a couple of people digging under a tent — we think they were archeologists. It didn't look like they were getting much done.

Now we are sitting under an umbrella in another caffè, and Z is having a glass of wine that has bubbles but isn't champagne, and I am having a pop, which here they call cola, and we are eating sandwiches made out of squishy white bread. Z is reading aloud how Miss

Hesselgrave chipped bricks out of the Coliseum to take home as souvenirs.

We are shocked. Miss Hesselgrave, you are a looter!

Thursday, July 11 — LATER

I have never in my life been so happy to see a bed! I get to rest my poor little feet! I will never think of shoes the same way again.

Tonight we saw the biggest fountain in Rome. It is stuck to the side of a building. The building looks normal (= normal for Rome) until you notice one side has a big pool of water in front and carved naked statues and splashing. Hundreds (I am not exaggerating) of people were there when we got there. All looking at a fountain. Strange, right?

So of course Z wanted to sit and look too, though for her (and for other people too, I think) *looking at the fountain* really means *looking at other people looking at the fountain*. Apparently it's a tradition that if you throw a coin into this fountain, you will return to Rome. I guess all the tourists tonight want to come back, because every one of them threw a coin in! Whoever gets the coins must be rich.

I threw in a quarter, which is not the money they use in Rome, but Z says it doesn't matter. She says it worked for her, and do you know when she threw her coin in? *1967!*

Z says Rome is different from how it was in the 1960s but not as much as you'd think. Back then, women had to wear a veil to walk into the churches, even if they were only there for the art and not the religious part. Even women who weren't Catholic had to wear veils. Now they don't. Z says this is a good thing because she was always losing her veil so she and her friends would have to take turns going in to see whatever famous painting was inside.

"There was a lot of that, too," Z said, pointing to two people near us at the fountain who were kissing so hard that their bodies looked pasted to each other.

To be honest, I found the kissing uncomfortable. But I don't think Z noticed my uncomfortableness. In fact, I am sure she didn't, because I had to say her name three times before she answered, and even then it was clear she was not paying attention. Her mind was somewhere else. I thought about asking what she was thinking, but she looked so preoccupied and serious that I'm not sure I wanted to know.

Friday, July 12

Our pilgrimage begins!

Today we are going to walk all the way to St. Peter's,

which is the most important church of our seven pilgrimage churches, which means it is the most important
church in all of Rome, which means it is the most important church in the world.

We are at breakfast now in the hotel because breakfast comes free with our room. Roman breakfasts are
intensely different from American breakfasts. All the
food is spread on a long table — many different kinds of
food because many nationalities of people stay here and
they all have their own kinds of breakfasts. So there is
cereal and ham and cheese and rolls and toast and fruit
and a thing that looks like pie made out of scrambled
eggs and other things I don't even know. And juice. Z
is having cappuccino and looking exceedingly satisfied.
She is figuring out how we are going to get to St. Peter's,
because the streets between here and there look like a
plate of spaghetti. I am having ham and two kinds of
cheese for breakfast, which I have never done before.
The people at the next table are arguing the way people
would in a restaurant in Red Bend. You know: quietly,
so no one notices. But they're doing it in a foreign language. Isn't that wild?

Even on the map, you can see how St. Peter's Square
looks like two big hugging arms. That's wild too, that
way back in Prophetstown, Wisconsin, on the other
side of the world, is a drawing on Z's bedroom wall

that looks just like where we're about to go. I wonder if there will be any old-man dancers.

Friday, July 12 — LATER

I have not seen any old-man dancers yet, but in these crowds it would be hard to tell. St. Peter's is not only the most important church in the world — it is also the most popular! I never knew so many people could be interested in the same building. We had to stand in line for a long time in the sun just to get in, and there were dozens of tour groups with guides who each had a different-colored umbrella so the people would know which guide to follow. Z kept following the guides who spoke English, but she did it in an extremely spyish way and would look in the opposite direction from where the guide was pointing so it seemed like she just happened to be standing there. Then she'd sneak a look at what the guide had been talking about as the tour group walked to the next place.

We have learned a great deal about St. Peter's but we have also been glared at.

Did you know that Michelangelo — the artist Michelangelo! — built St. Peter's Church? He was an architect too. Although he was not the only architect.

Many other Italians worked on it as well, including the man who carved the elephant we saw yesterday, who by the way is named Bernini. That is amazing to me, that Bernini could be good at elephants and churches both.

Michelangelo also designed the uniforms for the guards at St. Peter's — that's what some people say, anyway. And the guards still wear them! They look more like Halloween costumes than guard suits, but still, it is quite respectful of them to continue to use the uniforms of the man Miss Hesselgrave calls Mankind's Greatest Artist.

I need to stop writing because Z has had enough cappuccino for the moment — we are in a caffè, but we are leaving again.

Friday, July 12 — LATER

We are at another caffè and it is extremely pretty. Many buildings in Rome are pink. It sounds crazy, I know, and no one would ever use pink in Red Bend, but here it looks good. Other buildings are yellow and brown and orange, and not one building is white.

Okay, back to our pilgrimage . . . St. Peter's Church was huge, but Z said she could not talk to God there. I understand. He would have enormous trouble hearing her over all the other people praying and talking and pointing to art. Besides, we have six more churches to go to, and Z says they are all quieter than St. Peter's. Well, at least five of them are. We know what happened with Z and church number seven.

After going inside St. Peter's, we stood in another long line and bought tickets to go to the top of the church — all the way up inside the dome. Now I can appreciate how big St. Peter's really is! It is over three hundred steps to the top. And some of those steps are super twisty and narrow (I am not joking: an over-weight person could get stuck). There are patches in the building too, where the walls cracked and the workers tried to push the cracks back together again. Even the floor has patches made out of stone!

I had not thought a building could be patched the way you patch clothes. I was wrong.

Curtis would love those patches.

Then Z wanted to visit the museums — apparently St. Peter's has famous art museums — but my feet said, *No way!* So instead we walked back to our hotel. Now I am eating Roman pizza, which is rectangular instead of round. And you do not buy it by the slice: you buy it by the kilo. All the different flavors are on display, and you point to which flavor you want and say *okay* — or *sì*, which is Italian for "yes" although everyone knows the word *okay* — and then the man cuts it and weighs it and you pay. Z has spinach, and I have cheese. The pizza is good, although not as good as Red Bend's. She is drinking fizzy wine, and I am drinking fizzy cola.

At St. Peter's, none of the pictures on the walls are painted the way a normal painting is, with paint on paper in a frame; instead they're made of little pieces of different-colored glass called mosaics. From far away the pieces really look like a picture. It is like they figured out pixels hundreds of years before the invention of computers.

Up in the dome we were close enough to see the different-colored chips and see how the artists made them into things like flowers and curtains and angels. We were so close that we could actually touch the angels' mosaic toes. Z smiled and ran her fingers across them. "I bet the guy who made this had a really amazing girlfriend."

"A girlfriend with funny-looking toenails," I said.

Do you know what is on the roof of St. Peter's? A post office. I am not joking. So I bought a postcard and a stamp and I mailed it. The postcard is a picture of the inside of the dome of St. Peter's. You can't see the angels (they are extremely small in proportion to the whole dome, even if their toenails are the size of eggs), but you can see the gold mosaic and the light shining through the windows and the overall enormous fanciness.

This is what the postcard said:

Dear D.J.:

This is St Peter's, which is huge and beautiful. I am not sure it is my favorite place in Rome, because we have only been here one day. I will have to visit more places. I hope your basketball is going well.

Your passenger,
Sarah

I wrote to D.J. because I have been thinking about her a lot. D.J. would never be happy just being the girlfriend of someone who made angel-toenail mosaics; she would want to make angel-toenail mosaics herself. She is the kind of girl I want to be.

Friday, July 12 — LATER

We are in bed now. We kept walking after supper — although slowly! — and talking about how much we would like to live in a pink building, but only in Rome. Z asked how I was doing with Curtis.

"Okay," I said, although I am not okay. "I think about him all the time. I wish I knew what happened." I didn't mention how afraid I am of seeing him in high school and not knowing what to do or say. Afraid of seeing him with Emily.

Z shook her finger at me. "You can't let a boy define your life. This whole world is yours, and you are so smart . . . Think about him, yes. But not all the time! Any guy who doesn't want you isn't good enough for you."

The more I think about what Z said, however, the worse I feel. I know she was only trying to cheer me up, but my mood ≠ cheery. My brain ≠ cheery either. My brain is doing its super-rational thing where it points out cold, hard truths.

For example: there are obviously a large number of guys in the world who do not want me one little bit, who are not even one-mosaic-chip interested in me. Most guys, actually. Probably >99% of them. Maybe the fact that I don't want to be an angel-toenail-inspirer doesn't mean anything — not if <1% of guys would want my inspiration anyway. Maybe I just have to get used to the fact that I will be spending my life all by my lonesome.

Saturday, July 13

TODAY Z AND I ARE GOING TO BE SUPER-PILGRIMS! We are going to visit FOUR churches in one day!

I am having coffee juice to get ready. Z is having two

cappuccinos. I am feeling much less uncheery — the sky is too sunny for me to be sad, even about my uninspirational future.

The first church we are visiting is the one I'm most excited about. Mary is the mother of Jesus and one of the most important women in the history of the world. This church is called Santa Maria Maggiore (*maggiore = major*) because it's the majorest church for her. You know who is buried there? Bernini, the man who carved the happy elephant! And the ceiling is made out of the first gold the Spaniards brought back from America. You always read that Columbus discovered America, but you never know what he did with it — now I do!

Perhaps instead of becoming a scientist I should be a tour guide.

Saturday, July 13 — LATER

Did you know that the Maggiore church is in a foreign country — a foreign country that is not Italy? Seriously. There is a fence around it with Roman police on one side and different-colored police on the other. It is part of the Vatican — like St. Peter's, which we saw yesterday, only I was so busy writing about other things that I forgot to mention it. The Vatican is a tiny country for the pope. It even has its own post office. Italy has a terrible post office. Everyone says that the vatican post office is much better.

When Z and I first got to the Maggiore church, there was a tour group outside with a tour guide who was Irish. I've never heard an Irish accent in real life before. It is so pretty — it sounds like old-fashioned flowers. I could listen to it all day. Do you think if I become a tour guide that I'll sound like that? (I know I won't, but it's nice to dream!)

The inside of the Maggiore church is so beautiful — I like it much more than St. Peter's. The columns come from ancient Roman temples. I think that is tremendously wonderful. The church also has mosaics of sheep that remind me of the goats I saw from the train. There aren't any mosaics of goats. Goats would not make good Christians, I don't think; they're too stubborn.

Right now I am outside by a fountain while Z buys a rose to put on Bernini's tomb. Isn't that romantic? We must honor the great artists no matter what Miss Hesselgrave thinks of them. Z also wants to take a picture of the Oreos. Oh! I forgot to mention that earlier. The floor of Maggiore has extremely fancy decorations made out of marble. One of the patterns is black circles, and as we were walking on them I said, "Look, Z! Oreos!"

And she laughed and laughed and said, "I knew we were in heaven!" So now she's taking a picture.

There is one other thing too... Many important people besides Bernini are buried in this church, and some of them have tombs that are really decorated. And in several spots — to illustrate that everyone is going to die and so you'd better be good — they decorate their tombs with skulls. Carved skulls, not real human skulls, but it is still vivid. And even though the skulls are carved out of marble, they still have bad teeth.

Curtis would love those skulls! He loves bad teeth. Right now I want nothing more than to show him. Besides, no one in Rome knows about the Brilliant Outflanking Strategy and the fact that we are fake boy/girlfriends. I am extremely sure that no one in Rome would even care.

Saturday, July 13 — LATER

I am sitting inside our number two pilgrimage church for today. It was done by a woman named St. Helena whose son was a Roman emperor, so she was rich. Miss Hesselgrave says St. Helena murdered her daughter-in-law, but even so she likes her because St. Helena was born in England. Miss Hesselgrave says St. Helena is a *mother of the church* (although not, I think, a mother-in-law of it) for all her church work and because her son was so important.

Z agrees. She says these two churches = the Great Moms tour.

I am not sure it is appropriate for me to be scribbling in my journal in such a sacred place, but I need to write this down.

Here is what happened. As Z and I were walking here just now, we passed two college students carrying backpacks with guitars strapped to them. Seeing them, Z told me a long story about how she was living in San Francisco in 1976, during the American bicentennial, which was the year the United States turned two hundred years old. She really wanted to go to the fireworks on the Fourth of July, but she couldn't find a ride so she ended up hiking across the Golden Gate Bridge with a backpack and guitar just like those two students. It was so windy, though, that she worried the guitar and backpack were going to blow off the bridge — with her attached to them!

She told it really well — Z is a great storyteller — and I laughed . . . But then I remembered a story Dad tells us about when he was a kid, when his scout troop made a gigantic float of Washington crossing the Delaware for their bicentennial Fourth of July, and Dad was supposed to be General Washington. But on July 3rd (which is the day Dad tells us the story every year) he fell off his dirt bike and broke his arm so badly that he had a fever and had to stay in bed with Grandma Ann taking care of him. So instead Uncle Tommy was Washington and Dad never got to be the father of our country.

Dad's story is funny too, especially because you can tell he doesn't feel sorry for himself at all. But until today I'd never thought about what Z was doing on that day, and about how when her son was lying in bed hurt and sad, she was on the other side of the country watching fireworks. That's not where I'd want my mom to be if I was hurt.

Would Mary have done that to her son, Jesus? I don't think so. Would St. Helena? (Actually, I have my doubts about St. Helena.)

Thinking about this has put me back to being uncheery. Uncheery and preoccupied.

Saturday, July 13 — LATER

We are about to go into the number three church. My feet hurt. I cannot stop thinking about sad things. What does Curtis see in Emily? Why does he talk about her, and notice her posters? Do you think he thinks she's inspiring? That is depressing. Emily would never inspire me. She would not inspire me to do anything.

Here is what I would write Curtis if I was writing him:

Dear Curtis:

Today I've seen lots of marble skulls with bad teeth. It is strange that rich people would pay artists to carve bad teeth on purpose. What do you find inspiring?

From, Sarah

PS: Say hi to your sister. But you don't have to tell her about the skulls.

Saturday, July 13 — LATER

We are at lunch. The pizza tastes like it was made last year and the pop isn't even cold, but the restaurant has air conditioning and the menu is in English. We are near the Coliseum right now, which means tourists x tourists (= tourists^2). Hungry tourists will eat anything.

I did not like church number three. It looked like a birthday cake full of sculpture and carved shells and decorations . . . The church did have the heads of St. Peter and St. John the Evangelist in silver jars, according to Miss Hesselgrave, but unfortunately I did not see them.

Now we have to go from here to *another* church — the last one for today! — that is so far away we have to take the subway. I know that taking the subway is not what real pilgrims did one thousand years ago when they walked to Rome from hundreds of miles away, climbing across the Alps and sometimes freezing to death. When they finally made it here, they didn't say, "Whew, now we can take the subway." No, they kept walking. And Miss Hesselgrave and her companion never took the subway, and that is not only because it hadn't been invented yet. Miss Hesselgrave would automatically disapprove of subways, I just know it.

But we are not those kinds of pilgrims. We are the Z kind.

Z is looking forward to this next church. She says it's the only one (except St. Peter's, obviously) that she remembers from last time. How could you not remember the other three churches we saw today? But Z says she and her college friends had been to a lot of churches by then and after a while they all look alike. Also they'd had wine with lunch.

Saturday, July 13 — LATER

BEDTIME. I just checked in with Mom, and she said it sounds like we're having fun. I did not tell her about the heads in jars. I would tell Curtis, though, if he and I were talking. If the two of us ever talk again.

Church number four is called San Paolo Fuori le Mura, which in English = St. Paul Outside the Walls because it is outside the old walls of Rome. It is definitely not a church that a lot of tourists visit. The subway stop isn't even labeled "San Paolo," just s.p. basilica. If you didn't know what s.p. meant, you would be stuck. It is a not-so-nice neighborhood. People on the street sell socks and pants and cooking equipment — stuff that isn't bought by tourists. You can also tell it's not a tourist neighborhood because of all the dogs. Guess what: Italians do like dogs after all! Walking from the subway to the church, I saw eight people with dogs. The people looked Italian, but the dogs just looked like dogs.

Remember St. Helena, the possibly English possible murderer? Her son built a church here to honor St. Paul, because this is where St. Paul is buried. They kept making the church bigger and fancier, even in the Middle Ages. Then, in 1823, a workman accidentally burned the building down. It was a huge tragedy.

Miss Hesselgrave visited after they rebuilt it, and she said the new church is "beneath contempt" — those are her exact words. I have to admit the outside doesn't have the tingly feeling of some of the other churches I've seen in Rome. Maybe that's why Z remembers it, because it is so untingly. This church could be a library in Minneapolis. There were hardly any people either, just some parked tour buses that I didn't pay attention to because you see tour buses in Rome wherever the streets are big enough for buses.

But Z did look at the buses, and then she stared at them, and she grabbed my arm and pointed. Some of the buses had red crosses painted on their sides and wheelchair ramps. One of the buses had its door open, so you could see inside. The bus didn't have any seats. It only had beds — beds and IV poles. Because the people riding that bus were too sick to sit up.

Seeing that gave me goose bumps. Already I had goose bumps.

Then we went inside.

Like I said, there was almost no one there. But you could still hear people singing. The singers weren't a choir in robes like you'd have in Wisconsin, but normal people who were marching down the center of the church — normal touristy people, only some of them had crutches and leg braces, and a lot of them were in wheelchairs. One man was playing a guitar as they walked. Even though I couldn't understand the words, it was the saddest, most beautiful song I have ever heard in my life.

They were pilgrims. Real pilgrims, not interested-in-art pilgrims like us, or bossy sort-of pilgrims like Miss Hesselgrave. They weren't wearing brown or carrying walking sticks or hiking to Rome from the freezing

Alps, but that didn't matter. They were pilgrims who had traveled to this church because they had faith that St. Paul could help them.

When the pilgrims got to the main altar of the church, they all knelt down — even the people in wheelchairs who could kneel — and they prayed in another language, and then they sang some more.

By this time we were near the altar as well, sitting off to the side. I wished Paul was with us. He would really appreciate this music.

I looked over at Z. She was crying. I thought she was crying because the music was so beautiful and sad, and maybe she was. But she looked so depressed — she looked even sadder than music can make someone look.

I wanted to say, *Isn't it beautiful?* or *You're on a pilgrimage: it's okay!* or *Remember the Oreos.* But I couldn't, because at that moment all I could think about was Dad's broken arm and how Z had not been there for him. So I didn't say anything. Then we rode the subway back to our hotel and went to a little restaurant for supper.

We didn't say much. Z had pasta with smelly cheese, and I had pizza that came with an egg on it. A poached egg, right in the middle. But I didn't eat the egg, because that's disgusting.

I feel like Z has a lot on her mind that she's not talking about. I have a lot on my mind too, but I think Z has more. I keep getting the feeling that something bad is going to happen.

I did not ask if she saw pilgrims the last time she was at St. Paul Outside the Walls. I didn't feel like talking about them at all — I felt like bringing up pilgrims would be disrespectful.

I would write Curtis a pretend postcard, but I don't even know what to pretend-say.

Dear Curtis:

I feel extremely quiet.

Sarah

I am not sure I would say even that.

Sunday, July 14

Today Z turns sixty-four years old. I sang her "Happy Birthday" as soon as I woke up, and I gave her a card that I had carried all the way from Red Bend. She was tremendously pleased.

Today is also the birthday of the country of France. At breakfast the hotel restaurant was decorated with little French flags, and some of the guests had red-white-and-blue pins because red, white, and blue are the

French colors too. Everyone was in an unusually good mood even though we weren't in France.

"Today is the Bastille Day," our waiter said.

"I know," I said. "And it's also my grandmother's birthday!"

"To be true? How many of the years do you have?"

Z smiled and said sixty-four.

"Oh! You are too young — you cannot be!"

Then he went away, and I thought that would be the end of it, but a few minutes later he came back with the other waiters and they stood around our table and sang "When I'm Sixty-Four" to Z! And people from other tables joined in — even people who didn't speak English! Some of them didn't sing that well and the lyrics got jumbled, but it was definitely the Beatles.

Z cried. Especially at the end when our waiter sang, all jumbled up, *"Tell me the truth, and make it sincere, you're who I adore. I know I will love you, think only of you, when I'm sixty-four."* Z thanked everyone and blew her nose and kissed our waiter on the cheek. She tried to explain. "That song has many memories for me."

"Ah," the waiter said. "The music, it is . . ." He touched his heart and said something in Italian that sounded meaningful. Z nodded.

Now we are back in our room. Z is taking a bath. She is singing loudly: *"I would be useful fixing a plug, if your bulbs have blown. You could plant a garden in a flower bed, buy us a yard gnome, paint the house red."* Only she stopped at "the house," so it sounded odd. Odder.

As soon as Z is done with her bath we are going to walk to the next pilgrimage church. We are already five-sevenths done! After this next church we will be six-sevenths done!

Sunday, July 14 — LATER

We are back in our hotel room having a siesta. A siesta is where you nap in the heat of the day, but Z is not napping. She is staring at the ceiling. She looks like she could stare at it forever.

I am staring at the ceiling too, but it is the ceiling of my brain. It is good I have this journal, because sometimes writing stuff down helps me to figure it out, and right now I need all the help I can get.

Z and I just walked in the heat all the way to San Lorenzo Fuori le Mura and back (six-sevenths done!). *Fuori le mura* means outside the walls, the same as St. Paul Outside the Walls yesterday, which shows how important the walls of Rome used to be. They were put up to keep out armies of barbarian invaders. If you built something outside these safe walls, this fact was so important that they put it right in the name. The Roman walls are still there, but now they have openings cut in them for sidewalks and roads. The openings are pretty small, though. I strongly advise against driving an SUV in Rome, or you will find yourself stuck. But you will not knock down the walls, I guarantee: they are terrifically thick.

San Lorenzo ("St. Lawrence" in English) was a Christian man back in pagan Rome who was grilled to death. I would not mention this except that in front of the church is a statue of him holding a grill. I am not joking. The church is where he is buried. It is much smaller than the other churches we've been to, and tremendously old — so old that the front of the church has all sorts of old Roman carvings stuck to it, kind of like a mixed-up antique store, and the columns on the inside are even more jumbled than the churches we saw yesterday. They are different colors and in some places they're way too short . . . It's like someone said, *Now it's the Dark Ages and you have to build a church, and you can only use what you find lying around in the ruins. Don't worry about matching.*

This church had the best mosaic I have seen yet. It is a picture of the man who built San Lorenzo. He is holding a model of the church to show that he paid for it, but the model looks like it was built out of Lego bricks. I love that.

And guess what: ANOTHER OREO FLOOR! Which I pointed out to Z, and she got a huge smile. "Didn't I tell you this place was special?" she whispered. Actually she hadn't, but I understood her point.

But then something happened — something almost as weird and stay-up-late-thinking as what happened yesterday with the pilgrims in St. Paul. As we were walking out, we passed a tour group, so of course Z stopped and not-listened. The guide was Italian, but he talked in English, explaining how the columns on the front of the building had originally come from Roman temples. But then he started talking about the 1940s, how *this* was destroyed and *that* was destroyed and the frescoes — so beautiful! — were destroyed when that wall was blown up . . . because San Lorenzo was bombed during World War Two! By us!! By "the Allies" — which means Americans, right? Or possibly British, but probably us. The whole neighborhood was bombed for hours in 1943, which means that it doesn't really matter whether an American bomb or a British bomb fell on the church: the point is, this building was knocked down by the good guys. It wasn't completely destroyed, but the front of the church was, and the roof and ceiling, and some of the paintings and murals too. And it wasn't rebuilt until 1949.

So this church I like because it's so old . . . turns out in fact to be superduper young. Young as in the exact same age as Z! Younger than my elementary school and Z's house!

I know: parts of San Lorenzo are still old, and the back part, with its Lego model and yard-sale columns, was almost not damaged. But I think it is immensely unfair to trick people like that by making the front of the church look old even when it isn't.

I also do not like the thought that Americans destroy churches.

After our siesta, we are going to the seventh church — the last one! It will be seventh out of seven = *all of them!* It is the church Z never made it to. *The time got away from me,* she says. This is one of the ways Z and I are different. If it had been me, I would have made sure no matter what that I saw all seven churches.

I hope Americans didn't bomb this one too.

Z is still staring at the hotel-room ceiling. She looks extremely far away with her thoughts.

Dear Curtis:

Today is Z's birthday. We saw a church that was blown up, but they put it back together. I wish you were here so we could figure out how they did it. Maybe we could make a project about it for social studies —

Do people do social studies projects in high school? Do they make displays?

Probably not. And if they do, people like Emily probably make fun of them. And now Curtis will not be there to do the project with me. He will not be there to protect me.

Sunday, July 14 — LATER

We haven't gone to church number seven. It got too complicated this afternoon . . . We will go tomorrow. We will clearly never be good pilgrims like the St. Paul pilgrims in their wheelchairs, so it really doesn't matter if we take another day.

This afternoon, Z kept saying she wanted to buy herself something for her birthday. Roman stores do not sell clothes that look like Z, though. So she finally decided to buy some lipstick. She spent a long time picking the right one — I think she tried fifty colors. The sales clerk kept saying, "That looks good." I think it was the only English the sales clerk knew. Finally Z bought one.

Then she said she had to show me something, and she took me to another church.

Yes, I know: *another* church. When we still haven't made it to church number seven! Z said this church was different, though — which it was, because we didn't have to walk very far at all to get there. The number seven church you have to take a bus to.

This church — the one Z took me to this afternoon — had tombs all over the floor (or under the floor, I suppose), which you could tell because full-length people were carved into the floor stones — knights and priests and others who you couldn't even make out because so many visitors have walked on the carvings and rubbed them out.

No one but me seemed to notice the floor people, though. Z walked right over them to the back of the church, where crowds of people were standing with their different tour guides, and she motioned to me and pointed to a painting hanging on the side wall of a chapel so you couldn't even see it straight on. "Isn't it amazing?" she asked.

I looked at it. Which was hard, like I said, because the wall was sideways. The picture was a guy who had fallen off his horse, and another man was helping him up. "You can't even see it," I said.

Z kept staring at the painting. After a while, she backed away so other people could get close, and instead she sat in a pew, staring.

"Do you mind if I walk around?" I asked at last.

"Sure . . ." she said. She didn't even tell me to be safe.

As I believe I have mentioned, my ex-not-boyfriend

Curtis collects skulls, and I have taken pictures of the skulls in different churches in case he might someday be interested in me again and I might someday be interested in showing him. Santa Maria del Popolo (that is the name of this church; there are many churches in Rome that begin with "Santa Maria," so it's the last words you have to pay attention to) had skulls too, and skulls with wings. And a life-size skeleton mosaic in the floor. Beautiful stones of all different colors shaped into ribs and femurs and kneecaps, set right there into the floor.

But that was nothing. Because built into the wall next to the front door was a full marble skeleton. Life size. It was wearing a marble cape — seriously, the cape was carved out of marble, but it looked like cloth — and the skeleton was arranged in a hole in the wall like it was just sitting there waiting! Or listening. Or both. It had its hands crossed on its bony caped chest, and it was smiling. Skeletons always smile, but this was extra smiley. Trust me.

I will admit I took a picture, and I will also admit I spent many minutes watching other people's reactions. Some people would do a double take and scream a little. Children covered their eyes and/or ran away, and one little kid started to cry. Every single person reacted. It became exceedingly predictable. Then it got boring.

Finally I went back to see what was taking Z so long.

She was still sitting in her pew. She wasn't staring at the painting, though. Instead she had her head bent over her hands, with her forehead resting on the pew in front of her. She was rocking the tiniest bit. It looked like she was praying.

This is what she was saying:

"Fixing me breakfast, making me tea, shopping at the store. I hope you'll still like me and won't ever fight me when we're sixty-four . . ."

I sat with her for a couple of minutes. I was doing my best to look like nothing was wrong. "Z?" I said at last. "Grandma? Um, people are staring at you . . ." I shook her a little bit.

Z jumped and looked around. "Sarah! I was just reminiscing . . . Do you know who that painting is of? St. Paul — the same St. Paul as our church yesterday. It's by one of the best painters in the history of the world."

"Mmm," I said. The crowds were getting even thicker, and the tour guides louder. "Why'd they stick it there?"

"They didn't 'stick it' — Caravaggio meant for it to be there!"

Then she said — like I'd forgotten, although she's never mentioned it before! — that now we had to go to the Spanish Steps.

Luckily the Spanish Steps weren't that far. We stopped at a minimarket on the way, and Z bought bread and cheese and a kind of bologna that tastes different from bologna in Red Bend, and a little bottle of pop for me and of wine for her, and the checkout man even opened the bottles for us . . . and she bought a pack of cigarettes!

We've been sitting on the Spanish steps for a long time now. The Spanish Steps are a huge swirly outdoor staircase. Here's what's strange: they are not even Spanish. The French built them, but the Spanish embassy is nearby, so that's the name that got used.

If I was French, I would be irked at not getting credit, because I bet these stairs were expensive. Also today is Bastille Day!

Hundreds of people are sitting here. We are watching the sun set and men selling things, and everyone is taking everyone else's picture.

Z and I are nibbling secretly (you're not supposed to eat on the Spanish Steps, but people do) and drinking secretly, and I am writing. Z is looking at everyone. She is an excellent people watcher. Sometimes she shakes her head or says something to herself, but she doesn't talk to me, which is good because then I can focus on my journal words. Once she gasped, but then she shook her head again.

Z has smoked part of one cigarette. She borrowed a lighter from a man walking by. He didn't speak English, but smokers don't have to. When she took her first inhalation, her face looked like she'd been waiting for this for a long, long time.

She exhaled. She looked at the cigarette. "I can't believe I ever liked these things," she said, and she put it out. She dropped the rest of the cigarettes into our bologna-wrapper trash bag.

I am so relieved! That cigarette smelled horrible! Don't get lung cancer, Z!

Now she is laughing to herself —

Monday, July 15

I am at breakfast. Alone. Z is still in bed, but I was awake and hungry, so I came down. The waiter asked if my grandmother had a good birthday. I did not know how to answer. "We walked a lot," I said at last.

"Ah, good! Then you must eat the breakfast to finish the hunger!" He even offered me a cappuccino "because it makes the hairs grow."

"No, grazie," I said, because I didn't want a cappuccino and I don't care about my hair. I am not a hair-caring kind of girl.

Today we are going to church number seven. Then our pilgrimage will be complete. Although after what Z told me last night I understand a little better why she didn't make it there last time.

According to Miss Hesselgrave, church number seven is built on top of catacombs, which are tunnels where they used to bury people. It was quite a common thing in the olden days to dig miles and miles of underground cemeteries. Lots of important people were buried there, like the early popes and a soldier named Sebastiano, who became a Christian and the pagans got so mad that they killed him and then lots of people visited his body and that's why the church is called San Sebastiano Fuori le Mura (there's that "Outside the Walls" again. Although now I'm thinking that *fuori le mura* actually means "there's a lot of walking in store for you!").

I really want to see the catacombs. Rome has lots of catacombs, but the Sebastiano ones are the most famous. People have been visiting them for thousands of years. Literally. So there aren't any bones left, because people thought the bones in these catacombs were so holy that they took them away to make other places holy too. For example: at one point they decided to turn the Pantheon — that building we visited the first day with huge columns and a big dome — from a Roman temple into a Catholic church, and one of the ways they did this was by taking twenty-seven wagonloads of catacomb bones and putting them under the Pantheon's floor.

I am sorry I did not know this when Z and I were at the Pantheon. But at least now you can understand why I want to see San Sebastiano so much.

Dear Curtis:

The Pantheon has twenty-seven wagons of human bones under its floor. Today we are visiting where the bones came from. Last night was strange and confusing and scary. I am trying not to think about it.

From Sarah

It's good that I'm not actually sending the postcards I pretend-write to Curtis, because then he would worry. I would worry if I got a postcard like that.

Monday, July 15 — LATER

We have not left our hotel! It is lunchtime and Z is still in bed! I know we also have tomorrow to get to Sebastiano + catacombs. But thousands of pilgrims over hundreds of years have visited this church because they hoped it would help them with heaven, and Z needs to go!

She keeps saying she'll get out of bed soon, but I don't think she means it.

I even went down and talked to the woman at the front desk. She speaks extremely good English but with an Italian accent — I wish I could speak like that, actually — and she showed me how to take a bus right to the entrance of the *catacombe* (guess what that means in Italian). It looks easy, even for a fourteen-year-old girl from Red Bend who has only ridden on school buses.

I went back to our room and told Z about the easy *catacombe* bus.

I said getting fresh air and exercise would do us a world of good (yes, I know that sounded 110% like Mom) and that we really needed to finish this pilgrimage because then we would be official pilgrimage finishers and Miss Hesselgrave would be proud of us. I said I was sorry that Z felt so sad and I wished I could help more.

Z said that everything I said sounded marvelous, but she still didn't move. I think she'd been crying.

I would call home, but what do I say? That my grandmother has been crying and I feel really bad and I don't know how to make her feel better and I don't want to talk about the things that happened last night that's making her sad? What would Mom say to that?

Curtis would not be helpful in a situation like this. Also if you recall I am not speaking to Curtis, no matter how much I pretend-postcard him. Dad is in corn season, and besides, anything I tell him goes straight to Mom. No secrets between those two.

The best person I could talk to, I think, is D.J. Schwenk. If I called her, she would tell me ... (I am pondering) ... she would say that it's tough but my grandmother needs me. I need to take care of my grandmother.

I can picture D.J. saying those exact words.

I'm hungry. And Z must be hungry — she didn't even have breakfast. I asked Z if she was hungry, and all she said was, "I'm a terrible person." I'm going to guess she is hungry, because hunger always makes a bad mood worse.

The problem is that the breakfast room is closed and they don't have any other food at this hotel. Only breakfast. Which isn't until tomorrow morning.

If we're going to eat, we need to leave this building. But Z is not going to get out of bed no matter how much she needs breakfast and I need lunch.

I've seen kids a lot younger than me walking around Rome all by themselves. I have some European money (called euros — as in *Euro*pean!), and there are more euros in Z's bag — I don't think she'd notice if I took some. There are lots of places to eat around here for someone who knows five words of Italian. I'll tell the lady at the front desk what I'm doing, just to be safe — but I won't tell her that anything is wrong with Z.

Be brave, Sarah. Be D.J.

By the way, I would write down what happened last night on the Spanish Steps, but it's not something I want to remember.

Monday, July 15 — LATER

I did it! I am a WORLD TRAVELER!

I walked to a pizza place, and I pointed to a plain pizza and a mushroom pizza, and they gave me pretty much the sizes I wanted, and they wrapped it up and I said *grazie* and they said *prego,* which means "you're welcome" — and I absolutely looked like a world traveler. I did not look fourteen. I did not even feel *fourteen.*

I did it!

I was extremely successful except that afterward I got lost.

Luckily the area I got lost in is full of tourists, so no one notices if you're looking at a map or looking lost, and the area also has many interesting stores — so it wasn't that I was *lost* so much as I was *wandering.* That's how Z puts it when she gets lost.

That's when I found THE STORE.

It is a store just for paper and paper supplies, which sounds boring but it is not. Romans have the most beautiful paper and pens! And notebooks and journals and art supplies (whoever knew there were so many colors!), and they even have paper plates and napkins that are so much nicer than anything you can buy in Red Bend. If Mom threw a party using these paper plates, everyone would wash their plates and take them home and hang them over their mantles.

I did not buy anything, but I looked at everything, which was hard because I was still holding the pizza, which was now cold and greasy and smelly. But I couldn't stop.

I have almost filled this journal, and I will admit that I looked at all the blank notebooks and journals — there were walls of them, with pictures and pages and sizes that I loved — thinking that any one of them would be fantastic. But I don't think there's much more that I want to say about this trip. Certainly not enough to spend as much as I am sure those books cost.

It's fun to dream, though. Someday I will graduate from high school and be grown up, and I'll travel to places like Rome and I'll write about it in books like that.

Now I am back in the hotel room and it is evening and we have eaten all the pizza, and Z has taken a long bath and she looks better. A little better. She says she had a little too much wine last night. I agree with that. She thanked me for the pizza, and I said *prego*. She is extremely proud of me for being so adventurous and independent. She said, "You remind me of me."

There was a bit of an awkward pause while we both thought about how much I was not like her at all — not in the ways that might hurt people and hurt their lives.

That is a depressing thing to think about. I will not think about that. Instead I will think that, except for the depressing parts and the Z-is-so-sad parts, today has actually not been bad. I will never forget the first time I bought foreign pizza all by myself. No one else in Red Bend High School has ever done that, I bet. And I will never forget that store. Plus tomorrow we complete our pilgrimage! Z completes it after forty-six years, and I complete it after five days. I will be a successful pilgrim + catacomber. So what if we are not official dressed-in-brown or singing-in-St.-Paul's pilgrims — I am sure that going to all seven churches gives you a boost into heaven no matter what.

Tuesday, July 16

We are at breakfast. Our waiter asked Z if she was sick and needed the aspirin. We said, "No, grazie." I am writing in my journal right now — you should see the bump on my finger! Z says I am an inspiration to her. Those were her exact words. I am writing a lot, but I am not writing everything.

Tuesday, July 16 — LATER

We have not gone to San Sebastiano yet. Miss Hesselgrave would be deeply disappointed. So am I — but at least we are going this afternoon! Instead we did something that was a lot more fun, even if it won't get us into heaven: we went back to that Roman paper store.

Z told me to pick out a new blank journal for myself "for future adventures" — I will store it away until I'm grown up, as a promise to me — and I got gifts for everyone, and Z is also getting a journal — in Italian it's called a *giornale,* which means "journal" because Italians don't use *j* — and a fountain pen.

Here are the gifts I have bought:

1. A little blank book with graph paper instead of lines. The pages are long and skinny and it definitely ≠ a Red Bend school notebook
2. A pencil case

3. Fancy paper napkins
4. Colored pencils in a real tin box
5. Another blank notebook with an amazing cover
6. Pushpins that look extremely un-Wisconsin
7. An eraser: ditto

I have not figured out who's getting what — I will be honest and say that at least one of these things I want to give to Curtis. I just can't figure out which one yet, because I can't figure out which thing I like the most.

Now I am waiting for Z.

Tuesday, July 16 — LATER

We are not going to Sebastiano after all! I will not get to be an official seven-church pilgrim! I will not get to see the catacombs!

Darn it!

This morning, as I said, we went to the paper store, and Z took forever to pick out a pen. But she did, finally, and by that point it was lunchtime, so we got some of those squishy white sandwiches again. As we ate, Z kept looking at the pages of her journal . . . *which were blank.* That was weird. Then she said that she "wasn't up for" going to the last church! I kept asking *why,* and finally she came out and said, with a sad expression, that she wasn't going to make it to the Oreos. Those were her exact words: "I'm not going to make it to the Oreos."

In other words, she doesn't think she's going to go to heaven, because obviously she can "make it to the Oreos" if you mean Oreos literally. I bet there are even Oreos in Rome if you know where to shop. Real Oreos, not pavement stones.

I know Z has been through an enormous amount in the last two days — which I am not writing down why because I do not want to think about it, but I know she has been suffering severely. I feel extremely bad for her because she is my grandmother and I love her and it is not a good feeling when someone has been crying and you don't know how to cheer her up.

So I did not say that I was irked that we are missing the catacombs, because Z knows already that I am irked. But I also did not say, "Oh, come, come, of course you'll make it to heaven!" because at the moment I do not 100% believe it.

Dear Curtis . . .

Never mind.

Tuesday, July 16 — LATER

So, we did not go to Sebastiano/number seven, and we did not go to the catacombs, but at least we went to the church with that St.-Paul-falling-off-his-horse painting so I could look at it some more.

I know: why would a non–art lover (= me) want to do that? But the church was nearby for one thing (no buses! no *fuori le mura*!) and also I decided that if I'm ever going to understand Z, and a lot of things and people around Z, I need to understand that picture. So I asked if we could go back and look at it again, and Z said yes.

She didn't go into the church with me, though. We both understood she couldn't face it. She stayed outside by a fountain, watching people. I walked through the church by myself, doing my best not to step on half-rubbed-out tombstones. Then I looked at the painting for a long time — looked and not-listened to the English-speaking tour guides.

I have seen a lot of paintings in the past week. Roman churches are bursting with paintings. But this painting is completely different from any of them. For one thing, most of the painting is pitch-black, which is a strange thing to do in a painting. And even though it's huge, it only has two people in it — two

people and a horse. No angels or puffy clouds or ha-
los. In fact, the biggest thing in the picture is the horse's
butt (!). And the people in the painting look the way
that two people and a horse would actually look in real
life. St. Paul is lying on the ground, and the other man is
looking extremely concerned, and the horse is looking
just as confused but doing its best (good horse!) not to
step on anyone.

What's most amazing to me, though — and to the
tour guides who I was not-listening to who I learned a
lot from, especially the British tour guide, who would
sound smart no matter what he said — is what's not in the
picture. The reason St. Paul is lying there is that he's having a vision of Jesus — a vision so huge that it knocked
him right off his horse. The other man can't see the vision, though. Neither can we. Neither can the horse. We
can't even see St. Paul's face! Maybe he isn't actually
seeing anything. Maybe he is simply hallucinating. But
he believes he is seeing Jesus Christ. And the real-life St.
Paul believed it so much that he wrote all those books
of the Bible that changed millions of people's lives.

I even like how the painting is hard to see because
it's in a corner. You have to work to understand it, but
then when you finally see it you appreciate it more. It's
kind of like Miss Hesselgrave's sentences.

I can understand now how someone looking at this
painting could fall in love.

Wednesday, July 17

We are on the plane. We got up extremely early and walked our last walk to the train station, and now we're flying to Chicago. Then we have to go through customs and get on another plane to Minneapolis, where Mom will pick us up, and then we have to drive to Prophets-town to drop off Z, and then all the way to Red Bend! All in one day!

I used to complain about how far it is from Red Bend to Prophetstown — ha.

Z has her new journal out and her special expensive Roman fountain pen. She's staring at the first page like she doesn't know where to start. She looks at me:

"I'm going to write down what happened."

"Okay," I say. I don't need her to explain what she's talking about. We both know.

Thursday, July 18

Everything in America looks different — the people and the signs and even the trash cans. Isn't that odd? My seven (There's that number again! Pilgrimage churches . . . hills of Rome . . . days of the week . . . deadly sins — what is it with the number seven?) days in Rome have turned me upside down! Perhaps I was expecting things to be different in Rome so I was prepared for it, but back in the United States I thought that everything would be the same. And that, Miss Sarah Elizabeth Zorn, clearly isn't going to happen.

Mom and Paul picked us up — Paul came all the way from Planet Paul to be there. Mom said I must be coming down with a cold because everyone gets sick on airplanes. Normally I mind her feeling my forehead, but this time I was too tired to care.

The drive back to Red Bend took forever. Mom and Paul kept asking questions, and Z was telling them funny stories and describing the pizza and our breakfasts and the bossy tour guides, but I didn't say much. I mentioned the poached egg on my pizza, and the stationery store that I fell in love with. I said I found the store all by myself.

Mom sat up: "You walked around alone?" She asked me, but she was looking at Z.

"It was fine — " I began.

"You don't speak Italian! What would have happened if you got in trouble?" (*"In trouble?"* I thought. *Oh, I know all about that.*) "How would you explain yourself to the police? What if you got robbed?"

"Wendy darling, she wasn't going to get robbed — "

"How would you know? Where were you when this transpired? Was she carrying her passport? Was

she carrying cash? How could you let this happen?"
Mom frowned at me: "How could you be so irrespon-
sible?"

Well, that was awkward. Then Mom asked what we
did for Z's birthday, and Z said we'd had a nice quiet
dinner together. Obviously she wasn't going to mention
what really happened, which is fine with me.

After a while we talked about something else. I told
Paul about the pilgrims singing in the St. Paul church
and how much he would have liked it. I didn't say that it
was the saddest song in the world. Paul said he was glad
to have me back, and I don't think he meant just for the
rides with D.J. I didn't ask, though.

We dropped off Z. Just before we got to her apartment, Z handed me her expensive journal-notebook
from the stationery store. Every page was covered with
her expensive-fountain-pen writing. She put it in my
hands and gave me a kiss. "Keep this."

I took it because Mom was watching and I didn't
have any choice, and I thanked Z for the amazing adventure and I waved goodbye.

Once we were back on the road, Mom asked, "How
was the trip really?"

"I grew up a lot," I said. I didn't say anything more.
I mean, I can say St. Peter's is huge and I liked Maria
Maggiore and it's freaky how Romans put poached eggs
on their pizzas, but that's not *what happened.*

At one point Mom asked, "Did Z have any wine?" *Hmm, Mom, what are you really saying?*

"Sometimes. Everyone did. People drank wine with lunch."

"Did you?" As if a fourteen-year-old drinking wine with lunch could be the worst thing ever to happen. I had to laugh.

"I tasted it once. It was fizzy, but it wasn't champagne — it's a European thing."

"Oh, a European thing." Mom raised her eyebrows.

"Yes. It is. But I only drank pop. Which is a European thing too. I had pop with lunch and supper."

Mom didn't even really hear me because she was so busy with her next question. "Was it fun?"

"Parts of it were."

"Was it safe?" she asked. Again.

"Yes! Mom, I'm really tired . . ."

Then we were home and I sleepwalked into the house and fell into bed and slept for hours and hours and hours. Today I woke up extremely late. I had some breakfast — a boring American breakfast of Cheerios from a box; no more tables of scrambled-egg pie — and I washed my clothes. They needed it.

I am thinking about calling Curtis, but I won't. I want to ask about Boris, but I won't do that either. Boris is fine or he isn't; that is the way it is sometimes with science.

I am going to put this journal away and I don't think I'm going to look at it for a long, long time.

I have put Z's notebook under my bed, under my box of American Girl clothes. No one will ever look for it there. I won't look there. I will definitely not read it.

But maybe I should read it. Right? I mean, I know what happened — that's what Z talked to me about on the Spanish Steps on the night of her birthday — talked about and cried. But I have a huge feeling that there's more to the story than what she told me. The *giornale* will have lots more of the story, probably . . . But maybe I don't want to know. I am conflicted.

Thursday, July 18 — LATER

Z's journal is still there.

Dear Paul and Sarah:

I am writing this because you need to understand where you came from. Sarah, you deserve it especially because of our trip to Rome, and Paul . . . you will see why you do. I hope I can be honest. I have never been honest about this — not to your father or his father and certainly not to myself. I am terrible at explaining and terrible at apologizing — but I am very good at making mistakes! I hope that by writing this down, honestly, I will begin to make up for some of my mistakes.

Goodness, isn't that a depressing way to begin!

As you know, I was born in Two Geese, Wisconsin. Two Geese is a small town now, but it was even smaller in 1949. Smaller in a lot of ways. Good girls ironed their skirts and crossed their legs and did what their parents and teachers told them. Bad girls — well, no one talked about bad girls. Everyone warned us about bad girls, but no one talked about them. I didn't know what bad girls did, but I knew I never wanted to be a bad girl. Terrible things happened to them!

Grandma Ann had me and Johnny and Janie and Ruthie and then eight years later — oops! — little Tommy. (That's what "oops!" meant back then: pregnant.) As the oldest girl, I spent the first seventeen years of my life as a maid. A second mother. I washed and I changed (this was before disposable diapers!) and I cleaned and

I minded . . . I ironed enough clothes to cover Wisconsin. Who cared if a toddler's shirt was ironed? Grandma Ann, that's who. Grandma Ann and every other woman in Two Geese. Every woman and every good girl. (Possibly every bad girl too, but I did not know any bad girls then. I befriended many "bad girls" later in life, and some of them were remarkably conscientious about ironing. The world is full of surprises.)

Every girl I knew married a boy I knew. They stayed in Two Geese or close by, and they popped out babies like gumballs. I wanted to get married like everyone else, but I didn't want babies to pop out of me. Not immediately. I wanted to know what I wanted first.

And then I saw the Beatles. They first appeared on American television when I was your age, Sarah, and my life changed forever. This was music I had to have; this was an experience I had to be part of! I had three girlfriends in Two Geese who loved the Beatles as much as I did, and we would plot how to meet them and buy their records and marry them. Not necessarily in that order.

From the Beatles, I discovered folk music, and rock and roll, and Motown. (Did you know you couldn't buy Motown in Two Geese? I'm sure I've told you this before, but to this day I am appalled. The record store would not sell certain records because of the color of the performers' skin!)

I cannot say if it was the music or the era or me, but even before I fell in love with the Beatles, I knew that I could not remain in Two Geese. I could not live in my parents' home working as an unpaid slave (I did not phrase it like this back then, but I felt it) until I became the slave of the man I married. I had to get out. And the only way a girl — a good girl — could get out of rural Wisconsin was with beauty or with brains. Well, I didn't have much beauty, but I certainly had the will to study. I won a scholarship — beating a number of boys who had never once paused to think that a girl could actually best them in calculus and biology. (Sarah, you're my granddaughter!) All while also serving as president and corresponding secretary of the Two Geese, Wisconsin, Beatles Fan Club.

I left Two Geese for a fancy East Coast women's college. I spent my freshman year going to classes and attending student teas and ironing my skirts, all while listening to folk music and doing what I could for civil rights (which was very little, but at the time I thought I was making a tremendous difference — I couldn't wait for Martin Luther King, Jr., to thank Alice Zorn!). Oh, there was a lot of gum flapping back home about how the Zorn girl would get herself in trouble and how she was aiming above herself — but I didn't care. I was going to prove them wrong. I listened to so much Bob Dylan that

I practically wore out the album. We all did. We were all of us rolling stones.

The summer after my freshman year, a professor offered a tour of Italy for art history majors. I wanted that tour so badly I could taste it. I wanted it almost as much as I wanted Paul McCartney, the very cutest and most talented Beatle. When I was in Italy, I might even meet Paul McCartney! Italy was on the same continent as England, after all. We could meet in a Tuscan church while discussing the early Renaissance . . . perhaps he would even kiss me. In fact, I was almost sure I'd meet him somewhere in Europe. It was fate.

Every weekend night I spent baby-sitting to earn money for the trip. Perhaps that was why I had so little energy for the civil-rights movement; I was too busy teaching professors' children the words to "The Times They Are A-Changing." I talked my way onto that tour. Ten of us girls plus one fusty male professor who was probably very relieved to see us go to bed each night. I don't think he could have been older than thirty, but he certainly seemed old to us. Old and out of touch — he listened to jazz! He didn't even smoke. If he even realized the times were a-changing, he kept that realization to himself.

We visited Florence and Venice and Siena — the Italian cities of history and art. Our first day in Rome, we went to the Trevi Fountain and Piazza Navona and the Forum — all the classic sights. We visited St. Peter's Square, where that old man really did dance with me. I discovered a couple of other girls had also read Lillian Hesselgrave, and they adored her as much as I did. Grouchy Miss Hesselgrave — she would have been appalled by my impromptu St. Peter's dance. And yet in touring Rome "unescorted," Miss Hesselgrave did things that were equally radical and appalling. She did things no one else dared to do. We needed to follow in her footsteps!

We begged our professor to let us take the next day off — who wanted to spend a glorious sunny day stuck in the Vatican Museums? Not us! He agreed, finally — frankly, I think he was glad to see our backs — and so three of us spent the day marching through Rome, either ignoring the oogling men or oblivious to them, taking turns reading Miss Hesselgrave aloud at frequent café breaks. That's why I can't remember the churches — when we weren't drinking coffee, we were drinking wine! Three giddy college girls, mad with freedom and amused to no end by this bossy Victorian pilgrim. We saw St. Paul's (here's to you, Paul!), St. John's, Santa Croce, Maria Maggiore, San Lorenzo . . . but we simply hadn't daylight and energy enough to make it to San Sebastiano. Also, by that time I believe we'd lost our map. We vowed to finish the next day.

*The next day, however, we couldn't. We were sup-
posed to have a special guest lecture from a famous professor, an expert on the great Italian painter Caravaggio.
But the professor canceled — I believe his wife was sick,
or he had better things to do in July than speak to a
bunch of giggling American girls. So he sent one of his
students, a thin young man with light brown hair and
blue eyes and the softest smile. He spoke softly, too, in
wonderful English. I do not remember a word he said
about Caravaggio that morning, but I will never forget
his face as he talked. I was mesmerized. We all were.*

*You can be sure there was a fair amount of jostling as
to who would get to stand next to him and who would get
to walk next to him as we went from church to church to
see the paintings. I remember a girl from Virginia with
false eyelashes and a dangerous smile who had the honor
of sitting next to him at lunch. It was July 14, Bastille
Day, my birthday — I was eighteen years old — and several of the girls wanted to buy me a birthday cake. They
couldn't find one, however, so they presented me with a
cream puff with a ridiculously large candle stuck in it —
they may have pinched the candle from a church. There
was a fair bit of laughter about that. The Italian student
was delighted by this ritual, and by the song "Happy
Birthday."*

*Then we went to Santa Maria del Popolo — the very
same church that Sarah and I visited. I don't know if it*

was the painting or the cigarettes or my birthday, but there was most definitely an atmosphere! All of us silly American girls lined in front of The Conversion of St. Paul, and no sooner did this young man start talking than I began to cry. I tried not to show it, but I was truly moved. He noticed.

After he finished lecturing, he took me aside to ask how I was — he was deeply impressed by how the painting had affected me — and we began to chat about my birthday and other things, and somehow it emerged that he was also a Beatles fan.

You must understand that Sgt. Pepper's Lonely Hearts Club Band had come out the month before. It was the Beatles' new album, and it was . . . it was an earthquake. Nothing like Sgt. Pepper had ever happened in the history of music. It was crazy. I even took the album with me to Italy in the bottom of my luggage. Mind you, this was a huge vinyl LP, and we didn't have a record player — I had no way to play it! But when we were in hotel rooms, four to a room, I would take the album out, and we would gather around and study the cover. We would sing it. We all had it memorized. We weren't that bad, either.

On an impulse I decided to confide in this young man. I explained my predicament: after two weeks in hotel rooms, I needed to hear Sgt. Pepper sung by real

Beatles. Did he have a record player? He didn't; he was only a poor student — but he could sing the songs to me.

"But you're not Paul McCartney," I said — quite the flirt!

"No," he said softly. "But my name is Paolo. I am the Paul McCartney of Rome."

Well! From that moment, I was his. I was utterly, completely, engulfingly mad for Paolo Sanpietro, the Paul McCartney of Rome.

We were under the strictest of curfews — we had to eat dinner in the hotel, just to be safe! — but that night several of the girls honored love over virtue and helped me sneak out. Paolo said he would meet me on the Spanish Steps, and he did. He had a guitar and the loveliest singing voice, and we sat for hours discussing art and life and religion (we were both quite against religion's constraints) and singing our way through Pepper. He wanted me to explain the more obscure lyrics. I'm not sure how good a job I did — there are parts of that album that I'm not sure even the Beatles could explain — but I did my best. He hung on my every word, and I on his.

It was the kind of night you read about in fairy tales, when the fairy godmother grants the cinder girl one evening of happiness. Of course, fairy tales don't mention what happens later . . . but at that moment I didn't care.

I was in the most romantic spot in the world, with the tenderest, smartest, most interesting man I had ever met. Granted, at that point in my life I'd met depressingly few men — Paolo would have cut a wide swath through Two Geese — but even with hindsight, I can say he was special.

We were convinced we were in love. That we, after only a few hours, were already in love. Perhaps we were — who can say what love is? We must have sung "When I'm Sixty-Four" twelve times! And each time we sang it, it felt more like a love song. We made a pact that night that we, too, would be together when we were sixty-four. That we would be together when I turned sixty-four. Oh, it was so romantic. We promised each other that no matter what else happened (and what could possibly happen that would interfere with love?), we would meet on the Spanish Steps on the evening of my sixty-fourth birthday. "And I will kiss you and tell you you are beautiful," he said, as only an Italian can.

I truly didn't think I could get pregnant. Can you imagine someone so dim? A college student with glaring examples all around me — my own mother! — and yet if I thought about it at all (which I barely did), I thought, But this is Rome . . . He's so nice . . . I'm in college. *But I never thought to think,* Watch out for oops!

Grandchildren, I am warning you: love will make you shockingly stupid.

Well, I snuck back to my hotel at 5:00 a.m. to find six American girls waiting for me, desperate to Hear All. I hope I satisfied them. To their credit, not one of them later said I told you so. One girl wrote me to say I'd introduced her to true love. She was terribly sweet about it, all things considered. That letter I kept for a long time.

I didn't see Paolo again. The next day was more museums . . . endless paintings of fat ladies . . . and an afternoon in the Villa Borghese gardens. The professor must have suspected something, for he and the hotel staff kept an eagle eye on me. No more sneaking out for this love-struck Wisconsin schoolgirl, no matter how deviously I plotted. And then we left. Flew back to New York — far, far from my Paul McCartney of Rome.

I spent the rest of the summer waitressing, baby-sitting, taking odd jobs — I tried to make it as a typist, but no one ever asked me back. Whenever I could, I'd go to the clubs. The folk singers, the rock singers. I never met Bob Dylan (much as I dreamt of it!) but I saw so many other brilliant stars — too many to list. It was a wild time. I'd thought I could present myself as a hip girl intellectual, but New York was teeming with those. The one thing the city didn't have, though, was a girl from Two Geese! If people knew me for anything, it was that. Isn't that funny? I couldn't wait to get away . . . and then I couldn't get away!

That fall I returned to college, but the classes didn't

grip. Who cared about Greek archeology when soldiers were dying in Vietnam? My own brother was going to Vietnam! Your great-uncle Johnny was drafted into the U.S. Army. He didn't even attempt to avoid it. I tried to get him to flee to Canada — to become a conscientious objector — to go to prison — but to no avail. He was determined to be a patriotic American. Besides, I had my own problems. I denied it for months — months! — but by the end of that semester there was no hiding it: I was definitely oops.

The college kicked me out without a second thought. Smears to its reputation were booted at once. I had no choice but to return to Two Geese and wait it out, then give the oops away. Get it adopted so I could get on with my life.

The judgment from the people in Two Geese . . . I don't know how I survived it. It wasn't that I was pregnant — most girls I knew got married pregnant; Two Geese Elementary School was packed with children born six months after the honeymoon. It was that I hadn't made an honest woman of myself. That's what drove me crazy: even good girls could have sex, they just had to get married afterward. They had to pay for it. And whatever boys did . . . well, boys will be boys. That's what the people in Two Geese said. And now snooty Alice Zorn had gone east and gotten herself knocked up.

That's what happened when a girl went to New York. It's funny: everyone focused on New York City. Sin City.

I was so angry that I let them think it. I wasn't going to ruin my memory of Rome. Paolo was better than that.

I felt so trapped. It was winter in Wisconsin, and I hated going out, hated seeing anyone — I spent four months ironing. I think I ironed the carpets — there was nothing else to do! I don't think I would have survived if it hadn't been for Grandma Ann. Whenever I'd get depressed, she'd say, "Everyone has skeletons in their closet. Anyone who says otherwise isn't looking hard enough."

Up until the day he was born, I intended to give my baby up for adoption. I wanted to be an artist — a folk singer — an anything-that's-far-from-Two-Geese. If I'd stayed in Two Geese as a single mom, I would have been judged. Your father would have been judged. Now, looking back, I'm not quite so certain of that — I've met others who did it and were stronger in the end, and more supported by their communities than I would have thought. But I didn't believe it then.

I wrote Paolo, you know. We wrote many, many letters back and forth. But what was I supposed to say? I cherished that memory of the Spanish Steps so much — I didn't want to ruin it, and letting him know about oops would have ruined it for certain. How do you say "oops" in Italian? (I am sure there are many ways to say it!) Instead I hinted at it, as cautiously as I could, and read his letters backwards and forward to see his response. I'd say, "Do you want to have a family?" and he'd write that he wanted many years of freedom before that happened. It broke my heart. After a while I stopped writing; it was too painful. Then I lost his address. The last time I wrote him, though, I reminded him that we were going to meet on the Spanish Steps on the day I turned sixty-four, and he wrote back that he remembered. He wrote again after that, but I didn't have the stomach to answer.

Then Johnny died. Your great-uncle Johnny, my patriotic younger brother. He didn't even make it to Vietnam. He died in a car accident on an army base. It could have happened anywhere . . . but if he hadn't been drafted, maybe it wouldn't have happened at all.

Nothing prepares you for that kind of pain. Your great-grandparents died a little that day. First their daughter — the first of the Zorns to go to college — sent home in shame, and then their golden-haired boy dead in a car crash . . . I cannot imagine.

That's when Grandma Ann said she wanted my baby. She wanted a child to make up for the child she'd lost. The two children she'd lost, now that I think on it . . . because I was pretty lost too. She had three children at home; another wouldn't be that much more. I named the baby Robert Zimmerman Zorn after a man who'd been born not far from us, in a town not much bigger than Two Geese, who'd escaped to become the greatest folk singer in the world. The voice of our generation. If people wanted to think this was Bob Dylan's child, that was fine with me. There are worse crimes.

Grandma Ann loved your father so much. She poured all the love she'd had for Johnny into little Bobby. And other people kept their judgment to themselves. The Zorns had earned this baby.

I left Two Geese as soon as I could, and I didn't go back often. Changed my name to Azalea and never answered to Alice again — no matter how much your aunt Janie tried. I'll admit: sometimes I thought of Bobby as my son, but other times I'd see him with Grandma Ann and his uncles and aunts, and I knew he was hers. What was I supposed to do — take him with me to hippie, freaky California? A kid needs a bath occasionally. He needs a mom who isn't coming home from rock concerts at 3:00 a.m. A mom who has a car that works and an apartment with hot water, who's not falling madly in love with that British singer who's going to be the next Mick Jagger — I swear it, luv! A kid needs a mom who's not a kid herself. And by "kid," I don't mean young — I mean immature.

So, speaking of immature . . . I grew up, finally, a little. When your great-grandmother Ann got sick, I came back to Wisconsin to take care of her as she'd taken care of my son, and then I realized I actually kind of liked the place. It helps that I live in Prophetstown, which has always been wacky. I don't return much to Two Geese. It also helped that I fell in love with my two beautiful grandchildren. I have a friend, a wise friend, who says that even the most terrible parents can somehow become decent grandparents, and I am the world's premier example of that! If heaven is paved with Oreos, it's because they were laid by you.

You both know (Sarah knows; by the time Paul reads this, I'm sure he'll know) — that Paolo didn't show up on the Spanish Steps on the evening of my sixty-fourth birthday. I never thought he would. I almost never thought he would. Why would he — we met over forty-five years ago! We were two silly young lovers — devoted, yes, but silly too; the two go hand in hand — who'd completely lost touch as people do. As I planned the trip, I kept telling myself I was only going because of my birthday, and because Rome is lovely and spiritual, and because of Miss Hesselgrave. Because I wanted to do the pilgrimage right. I can only imagine Miss Hesselgrave's reaction, were she to learn the deep secret beneath my enthusiasm for repeating her journey — she might swallow a tea cup!

I didn't want to go alone. I had friends I could ask who would understand everything, but I couldn't bear that. If Paolo did reappear — if if if! But he wouldn't wouldn't wouldn't! — I wanted to show that I'd made something of my life. That I wasn't simply a ditzy American yoga instructor traveling with her latest divorced friend. But I didn't have much else to show to him. Yoga only goes so far. Jack Russell George doesn't travel well.

No, my very best accomplishment was my family. I don't know how it happened — I certainly had nothing to do with it! — but little Bobby had grown up into a wonderful husband and engineer and dad. He feeds millions of people — do you understand that? Do you, really? Thanks to Robert Zimmerman Zorn, I can say that I have helped the world because I created a son who does.

Problem was, I wasn't ever going to get your father to Rome. He won't drive to Minneapolis during corn season! He has all he needs in Red Bend. (Lucky man — he carries his peace with him rather than searching the world like a shell-less snail.) And I didn't have the courage to tell him the truth and present this crazy scheme to him. I didn't have the courage to present it to myself!

I decided instead to take my grandchildren. Paul, imagine if (if if if!) you got to meet Paolo — another musician! But how could I take you away from your music?

Besides, you have the peace of your dad — I could tell you had no desire to go.

Sarah, you are such a natural traveler — so level-headed and curious. You listen and you walk, which are the two skills a tourist needs most. Miss Hesselgrave would be so proud! So off we went, Sarah and I, the perfect travel team, and I swore I wouldn't even visit the Spanish Steps, though perhaps I'd tell my romantic story to my granddaughter, and warn her to protect herself. Protect in every way. Each day in Rome, I'd think that nothing would happen, that we were only in the city by coincidence, that this had nothing to do with your grandfather . . . Did I hide it well? I think I did. I certainly hid it from myself! And then my birthday, and the waiters singing that song . . . that's when I realized I had a lot more vested in this trip than I'd ever admitted. That I'd met Paolo after the sixth church. That I couldn't complete Miss Hesselgrave's pilgrimage until I saw him — until I had the chance to meet him again.

Suddenly I so desperately wanted to meet him again. I prayed to God and Caravaggio to make it happen. Sarah, when we sat down on the Spanish Steps, my heart was in my throat — I'm surprised you couldn't hear it beating! I'm surprised the handbag hawkers couldn't hear it!

Did you notice how I stared at every person there?

Especially men who'd be sixty-eight now, with light brown hair (or balding or gray) and blue eyes that I'm sure still make women weak at the knees. I knew Paolo wouldn't come . . . but I couldn't stop hoping. With every passing moment, with each dip of the sun, I hoped more. Forty-six years of hoping, let free at last!

And then he didn't come — why would he? — and I had to admit I'd made a mistake. I'd hung my heart on an ancient wisp of a promise, and now I was paying the price. Sarah, you were there: you saw how I fell apart. For a while I thought my world had ended. I tried to explain, but I don't think I did a very good job. I certainly don't feel I did a good job — all I felt was your confusion and your disappointment. You certainly had a right to disappointment!

I'm disappointed too. I'm disappointed in myself, but I'm also disappointed that Paolo didn't get to meet my wonderful granddaughter. His wonderful granddaughter! He may have granddaughters of his own — who knows? Men who claim they don't want to settle are always the ones who drop with a thump. You could have dozens of Italian cousins by now — cousins who appreciate Caravaggio. Or perhaps Paolo's not even alive any more. That's the horrible part of not knowing: you just don't know.

Instead I ruined your vacation. I've screwed up ev-

erything. You didn't get to finish your pilgrimage . . . but I could never have gone to San Sebastiano. Not after that. Not after I realized I was such a screwup. I know you're mad at me. Paul, you're probably mad at me too. I deserve it. But please understand that I didn't want to screw up. I just wanted everyone to be happy. I wanted to tie up the strings of my big hippie story with a big shiny Italian bow. Well, at least I'm consistent. I've been bungling things my whole life: why stop now?

I love you both very much, and I hope that some-day — maybe when you're sixty-four — you'll understand a little better what I've been through. Love is the hardest thing in the world. I know you'll both do it well.

Your devoted grandmother,

Z

IL GIORNALE

Friday, July 19

As you can see, I have started using my new journal. So much for saving this special Italian *giornale* for a special occasion. Although this is a special occasion if you consider it a special occasion to be losing your mind.

I read Z's journal. It was hard, but I did it. Actually, it was only hard at the beginning, and then I got into it. Then I was too busy reading. Now that I've finished, though, it is hard again. Hard^2.

If Z took what she just wrote — what she wrote in her fancy Italian notebook with her expensive Italian fountain pen — and turned it in as a school English paper, she would get an A. She would probably win a school award or a state award for writing such a good memoir. A normal person would read it and think, *Wow, this woman has had a remarkable life! Fooling around can have serious consequences! She really loves her family!*

Not me, though. Because I can see what is missing, and what she has blurred. She wrote a story as crisp as *The Conversion of St. Paul* . . . but Caravaggio left a lot out of his painting too.

Now I am irked. No, not irked: furious. Here are all the reasons why:

1. Z said she wanted to go to Rome to reconnect with God and because she liked Miss Hesselgrave. But Z didn't want to reconnect with God, really — she wanted to reconnect with Paolo! And she doesn't even like Miss Hesselgrave. Z enjoys Miss Hesselgrave, but she doesn't like her — no one does. Z lied to me!

2. Paolo didn't show up (I don't blame him — he probably forgot all about it. You'd do that after forty-six years). But what if he had shown up and had met his one-night-girlfriend-now-sixty-four-year-old-yoga-instructor and the first thing she says is "Surprise! Here's your granddaughter!" That is a surprise like having a bomb dropped on you is a surprise. (And I've looked up pictures of San Lorenzo after the bomb dropped on it — the church was in a million surprised little pieces.) She could have given him a heart attack! He could have run away screaming and slipped on the Spanish Steps (they're extremely slippery) and broken his neck and died! He could have pulled out a knife and stabbed us! Okay, that last one probably wouldn't happen, but you never know. Z never knew because she never even thought to

warn him. Just like she didn't warn me. Instead of a big friendly new-family surprise hug, we all could have been utterly traumatized.

3. But Paolo didn't come. So why did she even bother telling me about him? Now all I can think about are the cool Italian cousins I might have and the cool art-history Italian grandfather I might have, a grandfather with wonderful Italian English and blue eyes. I want to meet them, and I can't! I've been promised a gift I'll never get to open — I don't even know what's inside the box! I don't even know if anything's inside it! But now I have to sit there and stare at the wrapping paper forever.

4. Z's the one who screwed their relationship up. Did you notice? Paolo wanted to keep writing, but she's the one who stopped. *She never told him she was having a baby (= my father).* She only "hinted" at it. That is not a fair thing to do to someone, especially for something as important as a baby. If she hinted to me about how nice kids are in Italy and how we could be friends, I wouldn't immediately jump to "I can't wait to have Italian cousins!" No, I'd say that it would be hard to talk in Italian or that kids there probably have lots of friends already . . . and Z would hear that and think

I didn't want to meet my Italian relations. I don't know what Paolo would have done if she told him she was having a baby, but Z doesn't know either. He might have freaked, but he might not have. Heck, he might have moved to California with her and followed rock bands for ten years. The point is that she never gave him the choice.

5. What about Dad??? Obviously Dad knows about Paolo or he wouldn't have named my brother Paul. When we were little, Mom and Dad used to joke that Paul was named after Paul McCartney, especially when our Paul started playing guitar. But it turns out they weren't joking, because Paul McCartney → Paolo the Italian guitar-playing Paul McCartney fan → Paul Zorn. They just never mentioned that extremely important middleman who also happens to be *Dad's father.* Who Dad has never talked about! Once, when I asked Dad about his dad, he said he didn't need a dad because he had family enough already. "Too much," he said with a laugh, describing all his cousins and uncles and aunts. Why didn't he ever tell me?

6. What will Mom do when she finds out about Z's big fuzzy plan to meet Paolo? I know:

she'll freak. Look how she freaked when she found out I walked three blocks by myself in broad daylight in the safest neighborhood in Rome. When she learns Z really took me to Rome to introduce me to a grandfather who didn't know I existed and then spent the next day crying while I bought food so we wouldn't starve . . . That will not be good. Mom will disown both of us. She is good at legal forms. She could do it.

7. This sounds extremely petty compared with everything else on this list, but I still get mad that we didn't make it to all the churches. People keep asking me, "So, are you a pilgrim? Did you visit the seven churches?" (which, just to clarify, no one in Red Bend even knew about before I told them). When I say no, they always look disappointed, and I always feel guilty and embarrassed and mad. But what am I supposed to say? "My grandmother was really upset that she didn't meet a guy she hasn't talked to in forty years who, by the way, is my grandfather"? No.

I can't write any more — I have too much furiousness inside me.

Friday, July 19 — LATER

Paul is such a wuss! He knows I am 100% exhausted from the trip and not in a good mood and definitely not interested in going anywhere, including Prophetstown. Especially Prophetstown. I told him I needed some time to myself for a while. Those were my precise words: "I need some time to myself for a while." I even told Z when we dropped her off Wednesday night that I wouldn't be able to dog walk today. Jack Russell George can survive on his own — he has a tennis ball.

But Paul just kept begging me to come: "It was so hard riding with D.J. while you were gone! I had to talk to her! Please, Sarah? Please. Pleeeeeease."

So I had to go. I didn't want to, but I had to. Besides, I like riding with D.J. D.J. Schwenk is the opposite of Z. She would never trick someone into going somewhere for a secret reason, or lie to them, or keep secrets for forty-six years. D.J. is a true and honest soul.

I also — if I am going to be a true and honest soul myself — have to admit that I, just a little bit, wanted to find out what was up with Curtis. When I think about Curtis, I feel so sad that we broke up (or "broke up," although right now it doesn't feel like quotation marks; it feels like we actually did it). I miss him. He was my best friend. I wish I could tell him about the skulls and the catacombs and the heads in jars. I would show him the postcards I pretend-wrote him. Also I am worried about Boris and how we will manage that. We still have to work on Boris — it is like a divorced couple with their children. We need to be professional for the science fair. Right?

These are exceedingly confusing feelings, particularly on top of all my other confusing feelings, so I was glad to get a chance to talk to D.J. — at least I could ask if Boris is still there. I know D.J. said not to talk about the calf, but I figured just once we could make an exception, if I could figure out how to weave it into the conversation.

There was a problem, though — a problem I had not anticipated. D.J. was not talking. We sat in almost complete silence for the entire ride — silent except for little slivers of noise from Paul's headphones. I don't think Paul even noticed that we weren't talking. D.J. just stared out the windshield. She didn't even mention the postcard I sent her from St. Peter's roof.

I am pretty certain she is mad at me. She has every right to be, given that her brother and I (")broke up("). Or maybe she's mad that I didn't send her any

more postcards of my favorite places in Rome. Or that
I only sent a postcard to her and not to Curtis. Part of
me wishes I could explain about the Brilliant Outflanking Strategy and how Curtis and I weren't really going
out . . . But broken is broken, no matter what shapes the
pieces were to begin with.

"How was Rome?" she asked once.

"Okay. Hot."

"Did you learn a lot?"

I couldn't help sighing. "Not what I thought I'd
learn."

"Ain't that the truth."

We didn't say anything else.

Now I'm at Z's place, but Z is not here, THANK
GOODNESS. Her apartment is a total mess. I don't
think she's done anything since she came back. I took
Jack Russell George for a long walk — a Rome-length
walk, although now I appreciate walking in Wisconsin
because it is not as hot! — and he is sound asleep. I even
washed some of Z's dishes because they were spilling
out of her sink. She clearly has an enormous amount on
her mind. But so do I.

I wish there was another way for me to get home. I
don't want to ride with D.J. — not when she is so mad
at me! Stupid Paul — this is all his fault. I wish I'd never
come. I wish I'd never done anything.

Friday, July 19 — LATER

Guess what: I feel worse! I feel the worst that anyone has ever felt. I HATE MY LIFE.

I am home and in my bedroom. I never want to leave again.

D.J. and Paul and I drove back from Prophetstown. The silence was thick like soup. Thick like poison gas.

D.J. did say one thing as she was pulling onto our street: "I'm sorry I've been such a jerk today." She swallowed. "It's just that my boyfriend and I just broke up."

"Oh. Brian?" I didn't know what to say. "I'm sorry . . ."

"Yeah. Me too. But I've got this tournament, he's going to college . . . It wasn't in the cards, you know?"

"I'm sorry. It must be really sad."

"It is." She parked in front of our house and looked at me. "And I'm sorry about Curtis. You two really liked each other."

That is 100% exactly how she said it: *You two really liked each other.* Not *Curtis really liked you.* She said it as if she assumed she knew my feelings too, not just her brother's. Even though I have never once talked to her about what my feelings were.

I did not say anything, but inside I felt exceedingly

angry that yet another person was making guesses about Sarah Zorn without talking to me first. D.J. had no right to talk about how I felt! Maybe Curtis *liked* me but I didn't *like* him — not in the way that she meant "liked." I haven't boy-liked him. I've only liked him as a friend.

OMG.

OMG.

I have just been hit by an honesty bomb. A bomb as strong as the one that destroyed that church in Rome. This is what the bomb is:

Sarah, don't you get it? You boy-like Curtis.

You, Sarah Zorn, are a liar. All this time you have been lying to yourself. You have been lying to him. You have been lying about not being a boy-liker.

I think that in a way I've lied to Curtis as much as Z lied to Paolo. Yes, she was pregnant, which I am not, thank you, but she was a liar about her feelings and her truth in the same way that I am a liar about mine. I have been lying to the boy I boy-like by not telling him what was really going on inside me.

Here I am so angry at Z when really I'm as bad as her. Maybe that's why I'm angry: because deep inside I know I mistreated a guy just as much as she did.

But I shouldn't be surprised. I am her granddaughter. I had to inherit something.

Monday, July 22

At least now I know D.J. isn't mad at me. That is one good thing. One of the extremely, extremely few good things.

I had to go to Prophetstown again today. I tried so hard to get out of it — I said I was sick, which was not a lie because I am sick inside. But Mom said if that was the case, then I needed to tell my symptoms to Jack Russell George and he would understand.

Which he would not. The only language he understands is Tennis Ball.

D.J. and Curtis are both away at tournaments all week. Why can't I be good at sports instead of being good at math and chess and driving people crazy? (Driving people crazy is what Mom says I'm good at.) This meant Mom had to drive us to Prophetstown, which I can assure you did not fill her day with sunshine. I made Paul sit next to her. I sat in the back on Planet Sarah.

Z's apartment was still a mess. I walked Jack Russell George. When we got back to Z's, there was a recycling bucket full of wine bottles by the door. I guess Mom had noticed the mess too.

I feel 24/7 horrible.

Now that the honesty bomb has dropped on me, I can see that I boy-like Curtis so much! But why would he girl-like me back? Who would girl-like a liar?

When Curtis and I broke up, he said that he wanted a real girlfriend. He said Emily doesn't lie to people. So he should have Emily. He deserves to have a girlfriend who does not lie — not the way that I have been lying to me. I am not so certain that Emily doesn't lie sometimes, but I am tremendously sure that she does not lie to Emily. I just hope she doesn't lie to Curtis.

I am having a myocardial infarction of boy-liking. *Myocardial infarction* is the word for heart attack. That is how it feels, anyhow. The pain will be in my chest forever.

Friday, July 26

D.J. and Curtis are still gone. Not that Curtis's life is any business of mine, but I am writing it down for the purposes of thoroughness. He will come back and be with Emily, and I will have to go through high school all by myself, and I will have no one to talk to, and I will be so lonely that I will die like a houseplant that doesn't get water. I will wilt away to nothing.

Mom is irked by my bad mood. She does not hesitate to say this out loud. Dad would be irked, but he doesn't have time to notice anything but ball bearings and corn. I am glad that he is working so much, because:

1. I don't have to listen to him also tell me that I am in a bad mood.
2. I don't have to be mad at him for never telling me about Paolo.
3. I don't have to feel guilty and confused about whether I should tell him about the Spanish Steps and Z trying to re-meet his father. Z is obviously not interested in telling Dad, but is that right? Does that mean I shouldn't even if I sometimes want to?
4. What if I tell Dad and it is traumatizing to him?
5. What if I tell Dad and he says, *Big whoop?* He's already said he doesn't think about his father. What if I am making molehills into mountains?

I cry in bewilderment if nothing else.

Mom drove us to Prophetstown again. We didn't say much. Anything. She sat at Harmony Coffee doing paperwork while I walked Jack Russell George. I could see her at one of Harmony Coffee's little tables when I walked past. Z was behind the counter talking to a guy who had so many tattoos that his arms looked gray.

If Z tells Mom what happened in Rome and it turns out that I was keeping secrets — which is how Mom would describe it — then I am in big trouble.

But I don't think Z did, because on the way home Mom only said that Z was stupendously complimentary of my behavior on the trip. Mom said that Z told her I was perfect in every way. Mom said, "I wouldn't mind seeing some of that back here in Red Bend."

I ignored her.

I have a blank *giornale* from Rome that I want to give to Curtis. Is it appropriate to give a gift to someone you are no longer fake-going-out-with who is probably going to be going out with your boy-liking enemy? I would say *Let's still be friends* to Curtis, but I do not think that will happen. It would hurt too much for me. I am sorry we are never going to finish "Skeletal Taxidermy and Bovine Osteology: The Process of Discovery," but finishing Boris would involve talking to Curtis, and that would hurt too much too. Plus he will be too busy with Emily.

The *giornale* has a picture on the cover of one of

those Roman-church skull-and-wings carvings. I don't want to keep the *giornale* for myself, because it reminds me too much of Curtis. I don't know who else to give it to, and it hurts too much to throw it away.

Monday, July 29

D.J. is back. Curtis is not. Just noting.

I am extremely relieved that D.J. is driving us again. I have needed someone to talk to, and she can sometimes be a good person to do that with. Not always but sometimes.

I did not want to ask about Brian and their breaking up because that would cause her too much pain. She seemed to be in a pretty good mood, and I did not want to ruin that. So instead I asked how her tournament was.

"Okay. I made a basket." She grinned. "That's a joke."

"Oh . . . I've never made a basket." I did not want to talk about basketball, however; I had only been making conversation. I took a deep, deep breath. "D.J.? I have a problem."

D.J. drummed the steering wheel. "You mean Curtis?"

"No!" Automatically I looked back at Paul, but he wasn't listening. Planet Paul had swallowed him up. "This is a different problem. This is about my family."

And then I told her. I told her about Z growing up in Two Geese ("I hate Two Geese," D.J. said under her breath, not interrupting me) and how Z got into college and went to Rome and visited six of the seven pilgrimage churches and met an Italian man. How they sang Beatles songs and promised to meet again when Z was sixty-four. How Z didn't tell Paolo she was pregnant, and she didn't tell her parents or her friends or even the state of Wisconsin about Paolo, because Dad's birth certificate is still blank where the father's name should be, and how she and I sat on the Spanish Steps for hours but Paolo didn't come and Z cried and told me all about him. How hard the next few days were, and how she was too upset to go to the seventh church and how she wrote it all down for her two grandchildren (= Paul and me) to have a record of forever. How confused I am now.

D.J. whistled. "That is one heck of a story."

"I know. I think I would enjoy it more if it was not happening to me."

"Yeah . . ." She looked acutely sympathetic, which I appreciated. "What's your dad have to say?"

"That's the problem — I don't know! Obviously he knows about Paolo, because of Paul's name, but . . ." I stopped talking before I got to the words *Why did he let me go to Rome? Why didn't he warn me?* I thought these words, however.

"Wow," D.J. said. By this time we were in Prophetstown. "This is really heavy. I need to think about this. Wow." She let me out at Z's house. "Wow."

Now I have walked Jack Russell George and I am waiting for D.J. to pick me up. Z has left me a giant stack of Dog Days of Prophetstown posters. She wrote me a note too, asking me to put them up in Red Bend. The note is nice, but it doesn't say anything even remotely important.

Monday, July 29 — LATER

I am sitting in my bedroom staring at the wall. My head feels like it's full of ten thousand fireflies all blinking at once.

D.J. and I talked the whole way home while Paul sat on Planet Paul. Sometimes I wonder if he's secretly eavesdropping . . . but I don't think so. Besides, his brain is so filled with music that I don't think our words would even register. We'd have to make them into song lyrics for him to understand. Extremely sad song lyrics. I don't think I'm up for that.

"I've been thinking," D.J. said, almost as soon as she started driving, "and I think you need to talk to your dad."

I sat there feeling fireflies hatching inside my cranium. *What do I say? Why did he let me go? Why hasn't he asked me about it? What does Mom know? What if she doesn't? What if he doesn't? What if I tell him and he flips? What if I tell him and he tells Mom and she flips? Maybe they think it's no big deal to meet your mysterious unknown grandfather. Maybe they think it isn't a big deal when your grandfather doesn't show up . . . But then why haven't they talked to me?*

D.J. looked over at me. "You okay?"

"Yeah — no. You're right — I think you're right — what do I say to him?" I may have wailed this last part.

"The truth. That's easiest." She laughed a little. "At least it is sometimes. But you can't keep this inside you. It's not right."

We sat there for a bit, lost in our own thoughts. Did I even know what the truth was enough to say it out loud? I was certain that I did not.

"And another thing, Sarah . . ." D.J. took her own deep breath. "What's going on with you and Curtis?"

I slid down in the seat. Now I felt twice as firefly-y

as before. Firefly-y and heart-beating-ish. "Nothing," I said. "Nothing is going on with us. Not anymore." I gulped. "He has Emily."

"Emily?" D.J. frowned to herself. "Wait . . . is that the girl who always makes those posters?"

I nodded a sad little nod.

D.J. snorted. "Oh, please. You have nothing to worry about."

I stayed hunched over in my seat. My cranium was still full of fireflies . . . But, I will admit, some of the fireflies now had smiling faces.

"Sarah, you need to talk to him. He's not going to talk to you, you know. He's too much of a Schwenk. And a boy. And Curtis."

"I don't know what to say."

"I already told you."

"Oh. The truth?"

"Yeah. That one. It's not that difficult. He likes you. You like him. You don't have to win a science fair to know that."

"We came in third."

She grinned. "Same difference."

"You don't know what really happened." And she didn't. D.J. knows my grandmother is crazy and terrible at boys . . . but she doesn't know just how crazy and terrible I am too. Us Zorn women

and our epic romantic failures. Perhaps it's a ge-
netic flaw, like color blindness. I wonder if someone could map the DNA of boy-liking-blindness.

But D.J. deserved to know. After all the talking D.J.
and I have done and that extremely nice thing she said
about Emily, D.J. deserved to know more than anyone.

So I bit the bullet and told D.J. Schwenk all about
the Brilliant Outflanking Strategy and how massively
unbrilliant it turned out to be.

D.J. thought for a long while after I'd finished.
Then she laughed. "You're amazing. When Brian and I
first started going out, we did everything to hide it. We
would have died if anyone found out. But you two —
you intercepted that pass before it was even thrown.
Wow."

"Great," I said. I did not sound enthusiastic.

She looked at me — looked at me while she was driving. It was safe, but weird. "You have a lot to figure
out."

"Yes," I said. "I do."

"Talk to them. Talk to both of them. It's hard, but
it's worth it. Trust me."

This is why I am sitting in my bedroom with my
firefly head. I have to talk to my dad and I do not know
what to say, and I have to fix things with Curtis and I do
not know what to do. The only thing I know is that D.J.

Schwenk believes in me. And that counts for something. Right?

Wednesday, July 31

Last night I asked Dad if the two of us could go out for ice cream sometime. He was sitting on the sofa holding two beers to his temples, which is what he does during corn season. He doesn't drink them, he just holds them to his temples until they get warm, and then he puts them back in the fridge. It can't be pop, either: it has to be beer.

Dad looked surprised. Mom was in the kitchen, and she did that thing where she keeps doing what she's doing but her ears grow large.

"That'd be great, sprout," he said finally. "I'm kind of beat now, though . . ."

"That's okay." I was happy to put it off. Now at least I could tell D.J. that I'd tried.

Tonight, though, Dad came home early. I don't know if it was because of me or the corn or what. I hope it was the corn's fault. As we were finishing supper, he asked if I was in the mood for ice cream, and at the same time Mom asked Paul to load the dishwasher. Paul these days is so lost on Planet Paul that he didn't even mind;

he just started sticking plates in and humming. Sometimes I'm not sure Paul realizes the rest of us are still on Planet Earth.

Dad and I walked over to Jorgensens'. The sun was low in the sky, although not like a Roman sunset. I thought about mentioning this, but I do not have the type of vocabulary that can describe sunsets, and also I did not want to talk about Rome. I mean, I did want to talk about Rome, but that did not seem to be the most effective way to bring it up.

I got vanilla. Dad got fudge ripple.

"So how you doing, sprout?" he asked. Dad eats his ice cream uncommonly slowly. He says he does it because it used to drive Uncle Tommy crazy. It still does: I have observed with my own eyes Uncle Tommy shouting at Dad to eat faster while Dad laughs.

I stared at my vanilla. I have thought for several days about how to say this, and I know many ways to say it that would be bad: *Why didn't you . . . ?* or *How come you never . . . ?* But I did not know a way to start this conversation that was good. *Tell the truth,* D.J. had said. I took a deep breath. "I wish you had told me about Paolo."

There. It wasn't easy, but it was the truth.

Here is one enormous difference between my mother and my father: when Mom doesn't speak, it is because she is waiting for an answer. But when Dad doesn't speak, it is because he is letting the quiet tell its own story.

Dad lowered his ice cream cone and cocked his head like he was paying extremely close attention even though he wasn't looking at me. He didn't say anything.

I didn't say anything either, partially because I did not know what else I could say and partially because I had started to cry. Which was embarrassing because we were sitting on a picnic table in Red Bend Park and because I had ice cream, which is difficult to eat while crying.

"Oh, sprout . . ." Dad patted my leg. "What happened?"

"Z took us to Rome to meet Paolo because they made that promise forty-six years ago, and so we sat there for hours even though the Spanish Steps were really hot, but he didn't come and Z said she hadn't expected him to but she obviously had, and now I am exceedingly confused because I want to know my Italian family and why didn't you ever tell me?"

Dad sat there for a long time. Fudge ripple dripped down his fingers, but I do not think he noticed. "That's why she went to Rome? Not because of the churches and that Hesselgram pilgrim writer?"

I nodded. "Yes. No. Hesselgrave."

"Paolo . . . Jeepers."

"Paolo means 'Paul.' " I did not need to say this, but I did anyway. Possibly there is more Mom in me than I would like to admit.

"She was serious . . ." Dad was talking more to himself than to me.

Who was serious? Z? What was she serious about? . . . I did not say anything, though. I was trying to let the quiet tell its own story.

Eventually he shook his head like he was waking up. "Jeepers . . . Sprout, I'm sorry. I am so, so sorry. I didn't know that's what she was doing . . ."

"It's okay. I learned a lot, you know. I am not just saying that either."

Dad studied the fudge ripple dripping over his hand. He looked bothered, but not about the ice cream. "I believe you."

"Dad? . . . Who's Paolo?"

"I don't know. Z only mentioned him to me once. She was staying with us after Paul was born, helping — well, she wasn't much help. She was awfully discombobulated. I think the baby was really hard for her. Brought back a lot of memories." He started cleaning ice cream off his fingers. I gave him my napkin. "Z and I were sitting at the kitchen table late one night, and she told me about an Italian man who played the guitar like Paul McCartney. That his name was Paolo. That he was my father."

"And that's why you named Paul Paul," I whispered, finishing the story.

"What? Oh, no. That's the wacky part. We'd already named him."

I stared at Dad.

"Maybe that's why Z was so discombobulated . . . I never thought of that."

"So you named your son after your father without even realizing it?" My mouth hung open so much that I could have eaten an ice cream cone sideways.

"Yup. Universe works in mysterious ways, doesn't it?"

"Wow . . ." I exhaled. I sounded like D.J.

"You know, I didn't even know this fellow was from Rome — I always thought they met in New York. If they met at all. 'Paolo' — it's almost too much, you know? And you know, I'm not sure Z even remembers telling me. She has a way of forgetting stuff she doesn't want to know. Or at least forgetting for a long time."

"Until she's sixty-four."

Dad gasped. "Of course. The Beatles. That's what triggered this."

I started crying again, just thinking about my next question. "Dad? . . . What was Z like as a mom?"

"She was pretty much like she is now. Not so many wrinkles. She'd show up with presents and big hugs, and then she'd go away again." He put his arm around me. "Some people — your mom, for instance — they're born to be mothers. And some people are born to be grandmothers. Z was an eighteen-year-old grandma."

"It wasn't hard for you?" I whispered.

"Sometimes. Being a kid is hard sometimes, even when you're grown up — being someone's child." He squeezed me.

"I'm sorry." I'd never thought about it that way before.

"Don't worry about it, sprout. You'll be real good at being a kid. You already are."

Then the mosquitoes started getting to us and we walked home.

Thursday, August 1

I am sitting in the park, at a picnic table. There's a softball game going on between a tractor-repair company and the county EMTs. If anyone gets hurt, it will be okay.

Last night Dad said he'd have to tell Mom what he and I talked about and he promised that she wouldn't freak. The two of them were up extremely late — the lights were off in their bedroom, but I could hear them talking, which shows how much I was awake too. I will admit that this morning Mom did not do her what-if-you'd-been-attacked-by-flying-monkeys thing. But she was most definitely on the edge of doing it. Simply lying in bed I could tell she was thinking it. I did not get up for breakfast. I did not see the need.

So now I am in the park because the library is too hot and Red Bend does not have a Harmony Coffee and it is afternoon and so Mom will be back from work and I have no interest in flying monkeys.

I am still thinking an enormous amount about what Dad said yesterday. It is a huge relief that he did not know about Paolo — that Dad did not let me go to Rome to a Spanish Steps possible disaster. It is a huge relief that Dad doesn't think Z was a bad mom. She was no worse at being a mom than she is at being a grandma, and sometimes she is extremely good at that.

I get the sense that Dad is not going to talk much more about Paolo. He's got us and Z and corn. That's all he needs. He's Planet Dad.

I think that D.J. would be pleased. She would be happy that I told the truth and heard the truth — a truth I hadn't even anticipated! — from him.

Then she would say, *And what about Curtis?*

Curtis is a different planet entirely.

He comes home Sunday. In three days he will be playing baseball in this exact park where I am sitting now. He has been on his baseball trip longer than I was in Rome. I wonder if he's gone through as much as I have. Is that possible with baseball?

Has he thought about me?

Has he not thought about Emily?

I cannot tell which of those two I want more.

D.J. told me to tell Curtis the truth. But how can I do that when I don't even know what the truth is! When I think about boy-liking, all I feel is confusion. Confusion ≠ truth.

Thursday, August 1—LATER

Something tremendously strange and provoking to my brain just happened.

I was sitting at this precise picnic table thinking about Curtis and Emily and life, feeling 100% confused and horrible, when D.J. Schwenk came over with two other girls and asked if they could sit with me because they had just gotten ice cream (mint chocolate chip; strawberry; something with nuts) and my table was in the shade. These were her two friends who happen to be going out together, which I know because everyone in town knows it, because two girls going out together is an unusual thing to do in Red Bend, Wisconsin.

I said yes, and D.J. introduced Amber and Dale,

although I already knew their names, and I pushed my backpack out of the way and *Two Lady Pilgrims in Rome* fell out. I have been carrying Miss Hesselgrave around for so long that I did not even know it was in there.

Dale picked it up and laughed. "Miss Lillian! I love this gal! She was one rocking lesbian."

If this was a cartoon movie, my jaw would have fallen onto the picnic table with a thunk.

There was a long and immensely awkward silence. "I'm sorry," Dale said. "I didn't think that word would bother you."

"Lillian Hesselgrave was gay?" I asked. Then I realized how bad I sounded, so I added, "I mean, gay people are fine," which made me sound even worse. "Miss Lillian Hesselgrave? She couldn't be!"

"Why not?" Amber asked, looking at me suspiciously.

"Because she was bossy and mean!"

The three of them started laughing. Dale laughed so hard that she stuck herself in the forehead with her ice cream. That made them laugh even harder.

D.J. leaned toward me. "Lesbians are always mean," she whispered loudly.

"Hey!" Amber said, punching D.J. in the arm.

"See?" D.J. looked at me knowingly.

My face by now was as red as Christmas wrapping

paper. "It's just that Miss Hesselgrave is always so criti-
cal of other people and she's always listing how they're
being improper, and someone, you know, that way is —
was — would have been improper . . ."

Dale smiled. "Lillian never got the 'Judge not lest
you be judged' thing."

"I think I really need to read this book," D.J. said.
"I didn't even know there were gay people back then. I
always thought they were like TV."

"What?" Dale stared at her, laughing.

"You know: modern." D.J. grinned at me. I guess
she could tell that I had been sort of thinking that too —
not the television part, but definitely the not-in-the-
olden-days part. Miss Hesselgrave! Now I was going to
have to think about everything she said in a whole new
light.

Amber studied the cover, then studied me. "Was
Rome like she described?"

"No . . . There's a lot more going on in Rome than
she ever talked about."

"You can say that again," Dale said with a look that
made the three of them laugh more.

I did not laugh. I had too much on my mind to laugh,
even if I knew what they were laughing about. (Okay, I
have a suspicion what they were laughing about.) They
chatted a few more minutes and then said they had to
go and offered to buy me ice cream but I said no thank

you, because my cranium was now so full that I could not on top of everything else pick out a flavor.

As they left, D.J. told me that Curtis is coming home Sunday, and she gave me a significant stare. I said I knew and that I would see her tomorrow on the ride to Prophetstown, and now I am sitting here alone once again trying to figure out Curtis but I can't because I am too busy thinking about Miss Lillian Hesselgrave.

Why didn't Miss Hesselgrave ever mention that instead of being a girl + boy kind of person, she was a girl + girl? Or in her case lady + lady. Which as a math problem could also be written as lady x 2 or simply lady(2). Miss Hesselgrave spent all those pages explaining how Italians can't make tea and how Roman drivers always cheat you and how Bernini makes a good elephant but a bad church, yet she never mentioned an important part of her trip and her personality and her life.

Why didn't Z ever tell me either?

I need to think about this a lot more.

Thursday, August 1 — LATER

I gave up. I got a cone. Rocky Road. I figured it couldn't be any weirder than anything else that's happened today.

But it turns out I was wrong — again. Rocky Road is disgusting. Whoever invented Rocky Road should see a psychological counselor.

I have been pondering Miss Lillian Hesselgrave a great deal — at the picnic table and all through dinner, and now I am in my room.

For the first couple of hours I was irked with her because she is such a liar. Never once in her book does she mention that she is a lady(2), and that is an extremely important thing to know about someone, especially someone who spends so much time criticizing other people's behavior and being so intolerant of them. (As Dad would say, don't throw cans when you live in a glass house.)

But the more that I've thought about it, the more I think that Miss Hesselgrave — even though she is judgmental and intolerant and a Bernini-disliker — is not a liar. She admits all the time that she has a lady companion who she travels everywhere with. She even calls her book *Two Lady Pilgrims in Rome,* which is an enormous clue. She is just not as blunt about lady(2)ness as she is about bad-tasting tea.

I have also been pondering why Z didn't tell me about Miss Hesselgrave's lady(2)ness. Maybe Z thought I knew (clearly I did not), or she didn't know herself (impossible; now that I know, it is *so obvious*), or she wanted to protect me from inappropriate adult behavior (ha). But I don't think it's any of those explanations. I think the real reason is that to Z, the lady(2)ness didn't matter. It's not the part of Miss Hesselgrave that she wanted to focus on. She only wanted to remember the bossy pilgrim part.

It's funny, but figuring this out about Z and Miss Hesselgrave has made me feel like I understand Z in a bunch of other ways too. If Z was a bacterium and I was a scientist looking at her on a slide, I would say that I now can see her at 50x rather than 10x. That is how much clearer she is to me. Like Dad said, Z has a way of forgetting stuff she doesn't want to remember. Or, as in Miss Hesselgrave's case, ignoring stuff that doesn't matter to her. But she also has a way of focusing on stuff she doesn't want to forget. She's never forgotten walking around Rome in 1967 with her college friends, visiting Miss Hesselgrave's pilgrim churches. She's never forgotten dancing in St. Peter's Square. She sure hasn't forgotten her night with Paolo. She remembers every single detail.

Maybe Z never told anyone about Paolo because she wanted to keep that night in her mind. She didn't want to risk having that beautiful memory attached to other memories that were worse. She wanted that one perfect moment . . . the tingly moment, just like the tingly moment that Caravaggio paints.

Wow, Sarah, that is actually an extremely beautiful thought.

Thursday, August 1 — LATER

Tonight Mom and Dad and Paul and I had a big talk. Mom and Dad wanted to know what happened in Rome. What really happened. Not the egg on the pizza and Bernini's elephant. They wanted Paul to hear it too, because it's his grandmother and grandfather and family.

So I told them. Mom did really well — she was working hard, you could tell. Even though she got that face a couple of times, she never said anything. Even when I told about Z spending the day in bed while I went out and bought us food.

Dad didn't say much. But he did a better job of listening without twitching. I showed him the journal that Z wrote to Paul and me. Dad flipped through the pages and set it down.

"Don't you want to read it?" I mean, I hadn't wanted to read it, but that was different, I think. This is Dad's father. I'd want to know about my father.

"It's not mine to read," he said. "Besides, I've got all the family I need. Too much, sometimes."

"Hey!" Mom said. But it was a nice hey.

Paul didn't even pick Z's journal up; he just listened to us all talking. "Is that it?" he asked finally — after hearing for the first time about his grandfather — his crazy-universe Paolo-Paul name! "Because I've got to go practice now . . ." And he left.

I stared after him with my mouth hanging open (my mouth has been hanging open a lot recently).

Dad patted my leg. "Give it time, sprout. Give it time . . . You know, you handled yourself really well over there. Really well."

"You were very mature," Mom added.

Now I felt awkward. They were making it sound like the trip had been terrible — but it hadn't. It had been hard and it had been sad, but that's not bad. Right? If everything in life was easy and happy, how would you grow up?

Then Dad had to call work about a replacement part, and Mom and I were alone.

"Mom?" I asked. This was something I've been thinking about a lot lately. "Why don't you like Z?"

"What? Of course I like Z!"

"It always seems like you disapprove of her. You know, her food things and her talk about karma and how she tells stories that might not be extremely realis- tic . . . Is it because she never got married?"

"No! I like Z . . ."

I did not say anything. I will confess that it was a

great feeling to be the one waiting for an answer instead of being the one who was expected to talk.

"She's pretty loopy," Mom said finally. It was like she was figuring out her words as she said them. "She's charming, but she's loopy. When she turns on the charm, though . . . It's not something I can do. I think that's what bothers me. Here I am working so hard, and maybe I'm doing it all wrong. You know?"

Wow. Mom was jealous of Z? Jeepers. Jeepers^2. "You're not doing anything wrong."

"Thanks, Sarah. Thank you." She gave me a hug. It was an extremely nice mother-daughter moment . . .

And then she had to ruin it. Good old Mom.

"You know, Sarah, there's a real lesson in what happened to Z."

"Really?" I asked. Of course there's a lesson in what happened to Z! A floor lamp could see the lesson in what happened to Z. "What, Mom?"

She glared at me. "You know what I'm talking about. Z . . . and boys . . . and fooling around and . . . babies . . ."

I could feel my ears going pink. I tried to pretend they didn't, though. I tried to act like a worldly world traveler. "Mom, Curtis and I broke up. Remember?"

"Yeah." She didn't sound that convinced, though. "Good. I mean — I'm sorry. But . . . oh, you know . . ."

"I understand," I said. But what I thought was, *I*

don't want to make a baby with Curtis — I want to make a calf. Is there a lesson in that, too?

Friday, August 2

Curtis is coming home in two days.

Is it boy-liking for me to write that? Or is it simply a statement of fact?

I am so untalented at this boy business that it is almost funny.

I did not mention Curtis on the ride today to Prophetstown, and neither did D.J. I think that if she asked me about the truth and Curtis, I would probably start to cry. Or I would talk enough to fill a ride all the way across the country to the Pacific Ocean. And after all that talking, I still would not know what the truth is.

D.J. did ask about Miss Hesselgrave, and I told her as much as I could. I gave her the copy of *Two Lady Pilgrims* that was still in my backpack. I said Miss Hesselgrave would probably disapprove of her.

"What part?" she asked.

"Everything. When you play basketball, you show your ankles."

D.J. laughed. "I knew I should be wearing knee socks."

"Hey!" Paul called out from the back seat. "Are you coming to my show? You know, at the Dog Days of Prophetstown? My band is playing. I'm in a band. It's really awesome. Didn't I give you a poster?"

"Yeah, I think you did."

"I'll get you another one. You should tell your friends. I'll get posters for them, too. They can come too. It's going to be really awesome."

D.J. said that she might actually come, and Paul repeated that it was going to be awesome. Planet Paul definitely likes the word *awesome*.

I walked Jack Russell George to the park, but I was not an extremely good dog trainer. A dog trainer should focus all of his or her attention on the dog, but my dog-focus attention was <5%.

On the way back from the park we stopped by Harmony Coffee. This made Jack Russell George extraordinarily happy because he knows that the customers sometimes give him food. He was quivering with anticipation.

Z saw us and smiled a too-big smile. "Sarah! What a treat! No, not you, George." Jack Russell George was having a myocardial infarction at the word "treat." "Oh, okay . . ." She slipped him a broken cookie, which he inhaled, and then he sat perfectly still in good behaviorness. "Why, Sarah, I haven't seen you since Rome — "

"I told them."

Z's face went from smiling to sad to disappointed to thoughtful to sad again. "Oh. I'm glad . . . Oh, Sarah, could I have screwed this up any worse?"

Right then a lady came in for cappuccino, so Z had to go do that. The lady gave Jack Russell George ¼ of her ham sandwich. If Jack Russell George came to Harmony Coffee every day, he would be the diameter of a Shetland pony.

I was glad for the cappuccino-lady interruption, though, because I didn't know what to say. Did Z screw up? Well, yeah, but . . .

Z came back. "Your dad called this morning, you know."

"Really? What did he say?"

"He just left a message. How's he doing?"

"He's doing okay . . . You didn't screw up, Z. I'm glad about the trip. I'm glad to know about my grandfather. I'm glad I got to buy pizza by myself. I'm glad we didn't get to that last church, because now I have an excuse to go back. I'm glad I grew up a lot."

Z dropped her head. It took a minute for me to figure out she was crying. "I'm sorry," she whispered.

"Why?"

"Because I know how much growing up hurts."

"Yeah. But if you don't grow up, you can't be a boy-liker."

Z's head came up. "What? Oh...I get it." She smiled at me — a real smile this time. A real, big grand- mother smile.

Now Jack Russell George and I are back at Z's. He's in his basket dreaming of ham sandwiches. I am sit- ting at the kitchen table with a package of Oreos that I bought Z as a peace offering. If I do not stop eating them, they will be an extremely small peace offering. I am trying not to drip milk on my *giornale*.

Saturday, August 3

I have read many, many books in which the main char- acter has an enemy who is the popular girl and the two of them don't get along at all, but then by the end of the book they find out they have a lot in common and that the popular girl is secretly insecure and they end up best friends.

I find this kind of story unrealistic. There is a 0.00% chance that it will happen with me and Emily Enemy. For one thing, if Emily is insecure, she keeps that in- security CIA-level top-secret. Emily hides her insecu- rity better than Miss Hesselgrave hides her intolerance for Romans — far better than Miss Hesselgrave does. And if Emily did decide to share her CIA-level top- secret insecurity, she would do it with one of her also-popular friends. Or with a boy like Brett Ortlieb, but only to make him like her. She would never share it with me.

But it doesn't matter. Emily may be insecure or not, or popular or not. She can think whatever she wants and say whatever she wants to. She can watch me in the high school halls and the baseball bleachers, and she can criticize how I act, and she can even make fun of Boris and whisper to her friends. None of that is my concern. I am not scared of Emily anymore. I can face those hallways and those bleachers no matter what. Do you know why? Because I figured out three (3) key facts.

1. Yes, Emily is an extremely good boy-liker, but she does not control all the boy-liking in the world. No matter what she says, she cannot tell other people how to do it.
2. I am extremely sure that Emily would never go to Rome. She would say it's because her friends couldn't go with her or she doesn't want to miss soccer practice or Rome is stupid, but I know the real reason. In Red Bend, she is a big fish in a small pond, and that is all she will ever be. But I am not. I am a fish of the world.
3. Emily is not friends with D.J. Schwenk.

Here is what I need to still figure out, though: Why do I feel so weird about going to Curtis's games but I love going to D.J.'s? Why is that? Why am I so worried about looking like Curtis's cheering girlfriend when I don't mind anyone seeing me cheering for his sister, who I am definitely not going out with?

Yes, I don't like girls who behave like they don't have anything better to do than worship boys (= Emily). But I didn't worship Curtis; I was his friend. Hopefully in the future I can be his friend again. Maybe more than his friend . . . maybe. But definitely at least a friend. I want to be ≥ friends with Curtis. It is not nice to ignore a friend. It is especially not nice when I am constantly comparing myself with Emily Enemy and trying so hard to be different from her that I can't even figure out what it is that I should be doing. That is not being honest with Curtis, and it is also not being honest with me.

I need to focus on being a better friend, and doing what friends should do.

Sunday, August 4

Curtis came home today. He had a baseball game this afternoon. I went to it.

Emily was there, of course. With some other girls,

all of them with matching GO RED BEND! T-shirts and holding posters, sitting near third base and cheering for Curtis. Which is fine for them. They are free to do whatever they want. Their posters are not my problem.

Curtis ignored them, which I extremely appreciated. He kept looking at the bleachers, checking out who was there, like his mom and adults he knew, and little kids who are his fans. When his eyes got to me, he stopped for a second, and I did not know what to do, so I just looked at him. Perhaps I gave him a little shrug or a millimeter-size smile. Some sort of sign to show that I knew we saw each other and that I did not mind the seeing.

Curtis turned away quickly and fixed his cap, and then he punched his glove and shouted something to his team. I could not make out the words, but they sounded encouraging. He bounced on his toes too. I was not sure these were absolutely definitely positive signs that Curtis might not mind my being there, but I did not consider them negative ones. I especially liked that he did not bounce on his toes after looking at Emily.

The game ended. Curtis hit two home runs. I stayed in the bleachers even after the teams shook hands and most people had left and it was just parents waiting for their kids and Emily's group pressed up against the fence, calling to boys.

Curtis took a long time — perhaps it was not long, but it felt long — to pack up his stuff. He did not look at me, but he did not look away from me either. I did not know what to do, so I decided that I should do what I would if he simply was my friend, and that was to wait for him. Just in case.

Curtis went and talked to his mom — still not looking at me. I tried not to think that perhaps I should be leaving.

Then at last he walked over and sat down next to me. "Hey," he said.

"Hey," I said. "Nice game." That is what one normally says in these situations even if one is somewhat uninformed about sports (= me).

"Thanks. Thanks for coming. How was Rome?"

"It was okay. Hot." I thought about all the things I could say at this moment. I crossed many of them off my list, and then I crossed more, and then I ended with this: "Do you have time for ice cream?"

"What flavor?" he asked. He was so serious that I thought, *What if he's switched from chocolate?* Then I realized he was just being Curtis.

Being Curtis meant that I could just be Sarah. "When I was in Rome, I tried a lot of different flavors. And I tried new flavors here, too. But I think I'm going to stick with vanilla. How about you?"

"Chocolate. I'm still okay with chocolate."

"Chocolate can be exceedingly satisfying."

"You know," Curtis said, "everyone says 'very,' all the time. But you never do. You're" — he grinned — "you're very good at it."

"My grandmother says 'very' is very unvaried."

"Yeah, but everyone else is too lazy."

"They're very lazy," I said. We laughed.

"Emily says 'very' all the time."

Suddenly I was smiling so much that I thought my face would break in half like an old Roman statue. "So . . . ice cream? It's very good."

"No, it's not. It's exceedingly good. By the way, Boris says hello."

"Boris! I've missed Boris. How's he doing?"

"Another couple of weeks, I'd say. Hey, I found some really good brass wire — you know, for mounting him — "

"That's great. What's it look like?"

"I've got it in my bag, in case you — in case you wanted to see it and stuff. In case anyone wanted to see it . . ."

"I definitely want to see it," I said, because he looked so embarrassed. "I'm extremely glad you brought it with you."

Curtis smiled his relieved smile. "There's some

thicker wire, too, that we could use for the spinal column . . ."

"We'll definitely need thicker wire for that. Good point . . ."

That's what we talked about, Curtis and me, walking over to Jorgensens' Ice Cream: calf skeleton spinal column wire. Emily might have been watching us, but I wasn't paying attention.

Monday, August 5

Today D.J. actually asked about Curtis. "How are things with my brother?" was how she phrased it. "Looking up?"

I smiled. "Yes. Things are looking up, I think. I do not know where we're going, but I like where we are."

D.J. laughed. "That's a great way to put it! Can I quote you?"

I said she could. I tried not to sound too pleased.

"Hey!" Paul said from the back seat, like he'd just figured out we were there (which he probably had). He peeled off his headphones. "So, you're coming? On Sunday?"

"This is that dog concert you're doing, right?"

Paul looked hesitant. "Well, it's not just for dogs . . ."

"I know. I was teasing." D.J. grinned at him in the rearview mirror. "What time should I be there?"

"We're beginning at, like, five o'clock." (Just so you know, the Dog Days Festival starts at noon. But for Paul the first five hours don't count.) "There's going to be dancing, too. We're playing some dance tunes."

"Dancing, eh? Should I bring a date?"

Paul turned purple. "If you want . . . It's not going to be just dancing, you know. There'll be other songs. We're playing Z's favorite tunes. It'll be awesome."

"Don't — " I said. I started to say.

"Don't what?" Paul asked.

I wanted to say, *Don't play "When I'm Sixty-Four."* But then Paul would ask why not, and I would say because of what happened in Rome, which he knows about . . . but I don't think he gets it. He doesn't get how Z cried and how that song, well, *made* Dad, if you know what I mean. The song + the painting. And + Paolo, duh. If Paul plays "When I'm Sixty-Four," Z will start crying all over again, right in the middle of the Dog Days of Prophetstown. In front of D.J., if D.J. comes. Crying in front of everyone.

But I could not figure out how to say this. Paul looked so happy and so hopeful . . . perhaps it would be okay. Perhaps I was just seeing flying monkeys. Or perhaps I'm too chicken to prevent a catastrophe. I'll never know. Instead I said, "Don't let her down."

"I won't," Paul said. He spent the rest of the ride talking to us — well, really he was talking *at* us — about guitars and amplifiers and chord changes . . . I did not understand ½ of what he was saying, and I don't think D.J. understood even ¼ of it, but he was extremely pleased to say it.

It is maybe not a bad thing that Paul spends most of his time in headphones. He doesn't pay attention to other people when he's wearing headphones, but he doesn't pay attention when he takes them off, either.

Z has left me an enormous plate of Oreos. I am sitting at her kitchen table right now putting together a book for Curtis. It is not much of a book, actually: just the *giornale* with the skull + wings picture on the front that I bought him in Rome, and eighteen (18!) photographs of other skull + wings or bones or skeleton carvings from the different churches we visited. I am arranging the photographs in the back of the book so that he has the rest of the *giornale* to do with what he wants. Perhaps we will use it for our notes on Boris.

I also printed out a picture that I took of Z standing on the Oreo floor in San Lorenzo. She is pointing to the floor and looking happy — so happy that she could almost be in heaven already. I have put the picture in a frame for her so she'll always remember that moment.

Sunday, August 11

THE DOG DAYS OF PROPHETSTOWN!

This week has been so crazy! Paul and I have been staying at Z's apartment so we could help set up — we have been worker bees even though bees have nothing (I hope!) to do with dogs.

And then today the day finally came. It was insanely busy. I was insanely busy. I helped with the pooches parade and the puppy-ista fashion show . . . Jack Russell George was supposed to be a pirate, but he chewed on his costume so much that he looked like a shipwrecked Jack Russell pirate. Jack Russell George does not have a future in fashion. Or in yoga. I don't think anyone, dog or human, learned much from Z today about yoga, but the Downward Dog yoga class was still supremely fun. And Z laughed harder than anyone.

I was also a helper in the Littlest Bestest dog show. Littlest Bestest was kids under seven and dogs under fifteen pounds; it was absolute barking chaos, and I spent all my time untangling leashes from little legs. Little legs were everywhere.

I had just finished giving out the last Littlest Best-est team a MOST OBEDIENT ribbon, because those were the only ribbons I had left. Actually, we still had a box of them. The little girl asked if she could have a pink ribbon instead of a blue one. I did not say, *Do you know what obedient means?* Instead I found her a pink ribbon and helped lift up her Pekinese, who was definitely > fifteen pounds, and off the two of them went.

"Well played, Sarah Z.," someone said. I turned around, and there was D.J. Schwenk. With Curtis! Although I tried not to show the ! part and instead simply waved a little.

Curtis waved back and then — it would be interesting to analyze slow-motion video to see exactly how it happened — I lifted my right hand at the same time he lifted his left hand, and then I lifted my hand more, and before I knew it we were Palm Saluting.

"Hey," Curtis said.

"Hey." I smiled. Whenever we Palm Salute, I smile.

"Okay, then," D.J. said. "I will catch up with you two later." She grinned at us and walked off.

I watched her go. Then I noticed Brian Nelson standing not too far away. He used to be her boyfriend. He is so incredibly cute that even I can see it, and normally I do not notice people's faces much at all.

D.J. walked up to him as if she was still his girl-friend, and he did not look like he minded. In fact — they kissed! In front of everyone! Then he put his arm around her and they ambled into the crowd.

"Wait," I said. "I thought they broke up."

Curtis shrugged. "They decided to hang out a lit-tle more before he goes to college. D.J. said they don't know where they're going but they like where they are."

Did you hear that? D.J. quoted me! She said my words!!!!!!!!!!! She used me like a fortune cookie!

"Do you want to walk around?" Curtis asked.

"What?" I said. "Oh. Yes. Sure." We started walk-ing.

Curtis looked down Laura Ingalls Wilder Avenue, which had crowds and crowds of dogs and/or humans, and dozens of booths selling art and food and beer and homemade cookies for humans and/or dogs. At the end of the street was a platform where they'd had the fash-ion show. Now two clowns were up there with a banjo and balloons and a tambourine, playing kiddy songs for all their Littlest Bestest fans.

Curtis studied one of the booths. "I don't think I want to try the dog biscuits."

"They're supposed to be really good," I said, "if you're a dog. Z said they were."

"She tried them?"

"She tried the vegetarian version."

Curtis looked at me like he couldn't figure out if I was joking. Then he laughed and nudged his shoulder against mine. I laughed too.

Do you realize what we were doing? We were walking around just like a regular boy-liking girl and girl-liking boy! If you didn't know us, you might even think we were a regular girlfriend and boyfriend! Just like the other people who were walking around in their own boy-liking and girl-liking ways. Possibly even lady(2)-liking too. Some of the boy-likers looked like Emily Enemy, but not all of them. Not most of them, actually. They were doing it their own way. Like D.J. and Brian. Curtis and I could do it too, in our own way, if we were brave enough to try.

"Curtis?" I swallowed. "I think you're right. I think we should give up on the Brilliant Outflanking Strategy."

Curtis froze for a second. He would not look at me. "There are two alternatives," he said slowly.

I spoke slowly too. This was not a conversation that a person (= me) should rush through. It was important. I didn't want to make any mistakes. "I would prefer an alternative that does not involve lying. I would prefer the truth."

"What is the truth?" he asked. Still not looking at me.

I took a deep breath. "I would prefer to be your boy-liker."

Curtis frowned like he didn't know what I was talking about. Oh, wait — he didn't.

"That means I want to be your girlfriend," I added quickly. "That's what boy-liker means in my brain. Which is confused sometimes. But not about this." So much for not making mistakes.

Curtis didn't seem to think I'd made a mistake, though. He had a huge shy grin on his face. "Okay . . . Is it okay with you?"

"I think so . . . I'm not really sure what it means to be a boy-liker — er, a girlfriend. I don't want to do it wrong." *I do not want to do it like Emily. I do not want to do it like Z.*

"Me neither," said Curtis. And then he pointed, and said something I was completely not expecting: "Look! Your brother!"

The platform was still there at the end of Laura Ingalls Wilder Avenue, but the singing clowns had left along with their banjo and balloons and tambourine. Now four guys were up on stage, moving equipment around and talking to each other in a we-know-what-we're-doing kind of way. One guy was kind of heavy, and there was a kid with huge curly black hair, and another guy with a long gray ponytail had a black leather vest that you could tell was his dress-up outfit — that was Z's friend Larry, Paul's guitar teacher — and the last guy was Paul. My brother, Paul. He looked just as I-know-what-I'm-doing as the other three.

They took their time, I have to say. I never knew that setting up could take so long. But I kept watching because it was interesting and because it was my brother, and Curtis kept watching for the same reasons, maybe, and then I noticed Mom and Dad watching too. Mom and Dad were there! Dad had his arm around Mom's shoulders, and the two of them were looking at Paul like they could watch him all night. Like setting up was all the show they needed.

The band started playing. It was just like Paul said it would be: some music you could dance to and other music that wasn't really dancing but nice to listen to — the sort of stuff Z listens to — especially if it's a sunny day in August with a lot of happy dogs. Some of the Littlest Bestest kids had stuck around in front of the stage, and they were dancing even to music that didn't seem all that danceable.

Z was there too. She was right in the middle of the Littlest Bestests, dancing with them and a couple of other adults who also looked like yoga ladies. Z was wearing one of her loose, floaty dresses and a ribbon in her hair. If it had been me, I would have been exceedingly embarrassed to be dancing in front of a crowd of people like that, but Z told me once that when you love musicians you get used to dancing alone, so I guess she was used to it. Also she had just taught yoga to dogs, so obviously she is comfortable doing almost anything.

Z kept waving to her gray-ponytail friend Larry, who'd smile and wave back as they played, and she kept waving to Paul, who couldn't decide if he should ignore her or not. So he'd grin a little and then go back to his music. That's the thing: Paul was playing! A real guitar, not just an air one. And when the ponytail man sang, Paul sang too! It was only humming-type stuff like "Mmmmm" and "Yeah, oh yeah" but still: he was singing! On a stage! In public! On Planet Earth, not Planet Paul!

"I didn't know your brother could do that," Curtis said.

I shut my mouth, which had been hanging open like a trap door. "I didn't either."

Across the way, Dad whispered something in Mom's ear, and she laughed. He hugged her tighter. They looked happy.

Curtis and I watched a couple of songs, and then Curtis said he was starving and wanted ice cream. He asked if I wanted any. Normally when Curtis says *ice cream*, I say *yes!* But this time I just said "hmm" because I wanted to keep watching Paul.

"I could bring some back. What kind do you want?"

"Surprise me," I said. Which was a joke, because we both knew what I wanted.

So off he went. While he was gone I watched more people joining the crowd in front of the stage, including — I am not sure I would have believed it if I did not witness it with my own two eyeballs — D.J. Schwenk and Brian. D.J. was sort of dragging her feet and laughing, but Brian was smiling and pulling her in, and you could tell D.J. wanted to dance even though she was acting like she didn't. She was a good dancer too.

Curtis came back with two ice cream cones that looked — I will be truthful — immensely disgusting. They looked like he had dropped them in the dirt and rolled them around and then picked them back up.

"Oh," I said. "Surprise."

Curtis looked extremely nervous. "I thought you might like it. It's not bad . . ."

I had to taste it. I had no choice. I tried to look positive as I took the first lick.

Curtis was right: it wasn't bad. Now that I had time to consider, it was not bad at all. In fact, it was exceptionally not-bad. In fact, it was amazing.

I took as big a lick as I could without my teeth freezing. "What is this?"

"Cookies and cream," he said happily. "It's vanilla ice cream plus Oreos."

My mouth dropped open again, which must have been disgusting with the half-eaten ice cream inside. Why had I never before tried cookies and cream? Vanilla + Oreos is the best idea ever! "This is extremely delicious."

Curtis smiled a huge Curtis smile. "I thought you would like it."

"I am completely in love with this flavor . . . Did you know that heaven is paved with Oreos?"

Curtis laughed. "I didn't know that. But I believe you."

"You should." Then I did something I have never done before. I think my boy-likingness was kicking in. I leaned against him. It just felt right. Perhaps it is his baseball muscles or perhaps it is because he is so tall or perhaps it is because he's a Schwenk, but as the two of us were standing there, Curtis Schwenk felt like something extremely safe to lean on. Something supportive, in every single sense of that word.

The guys on stage finished a song and whispered for a minute. There were more people dancing now, grownups as well as kids, although I could still see Z right in the front, and D.J. and Brian off to one side. Up on stage, Paul was shaking his head as the ponytail man was nodding at him. Paul didn't look like a concentrating, I-know-what-I'm-doing musician anymore. He looked like normal Paul. But right in the middle of their talking, the ponytail man turned to the microphone: "Folks, lemme introduce Paul Zorn. Paul?"

Uh-oh, I thought. I stood up straight. Curtis stood straighter too.

Paul took a deep breath and looked at the microphone. He gulped. "Hey. I, um . . . I . . . this next song is for my grandma. Azalea Zorn. It's her favorite."

Z's back was to me. I couldn't tell if she was happy or sad or scared. *Please,* I thought, *please do not lose it in front of everyone. Everyone turns sixty-four sometime. It's just a song.*

Paul gulped again. "And, um, Z? One other thing. Larry thinks you're one hot mama." Then he put his head down and began to play.

The crowd cracked up. Everyone could tell Paul isn't the kind of kid who says things like "hot mama." Even the people who did not know him — which = almost everyone — even they laughed.

I didn't laugh, though. I was far too worried about what was coming next.

Larry the ponytail man made a face at Paul, but then he started to play too. And then the first notes came out, and Z covered her mouth.

It was not "When I'm Sixty-Four." It was a different song entirely.

You know the drawing of St. Peter's Square that

Z has in her bedroom, and how she has it there because it reminds her of Rome? Well, right next to it
is a picture of a buffalo skull with huge black wings
behind it. It's not actually a picture: it's an album
cover she put in a frame. It's from a band called the
Eagles, which is kind of like the Beatles but at least
they spelled the animal's name right, and Z listened to
them a lot when she lived in California. She listened
to them for years, and she went to a bunch of their
concerts.

Z doesn't say much about the buffalo-skull picture — not like we talk about the drawing of St. Peter's
Square. She just says the album has a lot of memories for
her. I know Z loves those songs — loves them so much
that she and Paul made up their own lyrics just like they
did with "When I'm Sixty-Four." I've even heard Paul
practicing Eagles songs this summer. But I never heard
him sing, which is what he was doing at that moment.
Singing in public. In front of hundreds of people, and
his Eagles-fan grandmother.

Paul wasn't just humming, either: he was singing
the words. The main words — well, the Z + Paul words,
which are different from the official lyrics but even better, I think. He had his eyes shut, which at that moment
just floored me, that he could play his guitar without
looking — it was like he was showing off. But he wasn't
showing off. He was just really, really focused. The two

other guitarists joined in, their voices knitting in with his, the drums pulling it together.

This is what Paul sang:

> *As I sit in the dark watching dawn come,*
> *As the shadows all lighten in hue,*
> *I remember someone who adored me*
> *Could it be you?*

The song was slow and sad, and Paul's voice was high and sweet . . . He sounded like he'd been born to sing it. Like the words and music both were written just for Z.

Some people started slow-dancing — the Littlest Bestests didn't know what to make of it, you could tell, but the adults did. The teens. D.J. and Brian.

Z didn't move, though. She just stood there in the middle of the crowd with her hands over her mouth. It was good that Paul had his eyes closed, because if he'd seen her . . . How could you sing, seeing that?

"For me, you know, life goes by," Paul sang. The three other guys joined in: *"Hope is better than a frown."*

Gray-ponytail Larry was watching Z, I could see. Slowly he stopped playing and set his guitar down.

> *Wish Fate had treated me well*
> *Wish I hadn't been such a clown.*

Now the hope that's left in me . . .
brings me further down, and turned around,
and further down some more . . .

Gray-ponytail Larry climbed down off the stage. He held out a hand to Z. She smiled at him and took his hand. They started to dance.

"Curtis?" I put my right hand up. I was whispering so softly that I wasn't even sure he heard me. I was whispering to his T-shirt, not to him. Then I put my left hand up too. "Would you dance with me?"

Only Curtis did hear, because he put his left hand against my right hand, and his right against my left, and I put my forehead against his T-shirt, and we moved together. Not dancing, really, because unlike D.J. I truly cannot dance, and Curtis never has danced once that I know of, but we were together. Together in a boy-liking/girl-liking kind of way. The way that people can be, if that's what they choose to do. We danced, and we listened to Paul sing about love and freedom and having faith even when it's hard to believe.

It was getting to the end of the song. *"Please give me one more journey, please make it be mine, please take it to the limit of the line."* Paul's voice got higher and higher with each word, his voice climbing above the backup singing of the huge-curly-hair boy. *"Take it to the limit . . . take it to the limit . . . take it to the limit of the line."*

The song faded into quiet.

The quiet faded into applause.

"That was awesome," Paul said. His voice came as a shock after all that emotion. "We're going to take a break now, but then, you know, we'll do more . . ."

I kept my head against Curtis's shirt. Around us, people were talking and laughing, and dogs were barking in the distance. It felt so good to have my forehead against his T-shirt. I could hear his heart.

We kept swaying together in our boy-liking/girl-liking kind of way. "This is nice," I whispered.

"I know," Curtis whispered. "Let's keep dancing."

"Let's keep dancing," I said. So we did.

Acknowledgments

Lillian Hesselgrave, alas, does not exist, although she should; luckily many other Victorians published colorful descriptions of their experiences in Rome. My favorite present-day writer is Mauro Lucentini, whose Rome is one of the joys of my life. Don't visit the city without it. I owe a great debt to Greg Severson of Lakeside Foods in New Richmond, Wisconsin, who patiently explained the food-canning process; to Deborah Lane-Olson, who did the same with paralegals; and to Sonya Lindgren, who summarized travel baseball. Mari Caplan, my co–lady pilgrim in Rome, enthused about every site we visited and even *let me read my guidebooks aloud* — a better travel companion could not exist. Thanks to Mom, Dad, Nick and Liz for critiquing so thoughtfully (Liz, that whole heroine-journey business: awesome); to my editor Margaret Raymo for once again shaping a lumpy manuscript into something readable; and to my agent Jill Grinberg for coaxing this passionate wisp of an idea through to publication. Most of all, thanks to James, who is an even better listener than he is a photographer. I will never forget the dusk we shared at San Lorenzo watching starlings calligraph the sky.